D0405500

CASE FILE 13
ZOMBIE KID

To the real Nick and Carter. You guys rock!

Case File 13: Zombie Kid
 For information address HarperCollins Children's Books, a division of HarperCollins Publishers, 195 Broadway, New York, NY 10007.
www.harpercollinschildrens.com

Library of Congress Cataloging-in-Publication Data is available.
ISBN 978-0-06-213325-0

Typography by Ken Crossland and Sarah Nichole Kaufman
17 PC/RRDH 10 9 8 7 6 5 4

First Edition

ZOMBIE KID

J. SCOTT SAVAGE

HARPER
An Imprint of HarperCollins*Publishers*

A Word of Welcome . . . and Warning

Please relax and make yourself comfortable. I always say nothing goes with a good story like a cozy chair, a soft couch, or a fluffy pillow. I apologize in advance for interrupting your reading. I'm certain you didn't open this book expecting to hear from an old man. And trust me, I am much older than you can possibly imagine.

But this isn't about me. It's about you, the person reading these words or listening as someone reads them to you. You seem a good sort. Intelligent. Funny. Better-looking than most. But not prone to bragging about it.

And yet the very fact that you hold this volume in your hands—that you dared open the pages of what could prove to be a rather frightening tale—tells me something about you. You are the kind of person who walks past graveyards, late at night, hoping for a glimpse of something gliding secretively among the headstones. While others lie awake in the darkness, terrified of unearthly beings oozing up from under their beds or slinking out of their closets, you dream of finding just such a creature. Capturing it. Perhaps taming it, as much as such a thing can be tamed, and making it your pet.

You are a lover of all things strange and frightening. Instead of running from what goes bump in the wee hours of the night, you search for it.

You remind me of three boys.

Their case, file number 13, is so incredible, so *shocking*, you may not believe it.

But then, it might be better if you don't believe it. You're probably safer that way.

"What's taking so long in there? Did you fall in?" Carter Benson called to the closed bathroom door. The only answer was a muffled something from the other side that he couldn't understand.

Stretched out on a big, red beanbag chair, in his friend Nick Braithwaite's bedroom, Carter scarfed a handful of Doritos and burst into song. "Stranded on the toilet bowl. What do you do if you can't reach the roll?"

"You are one sick tadpole," Angelo Ruiz said without looking up from Nick's desk, where he was putting the finishing touches on a very realistic-looking plastic vampire model.

"He's been in there half an hour," Carter said around a mouthful of chips. "Even my sister doesn't take that long. Kid ought to try prune juice or something."

Angelo pushed back the dark hair hanging in his eyes, added two drops of red paint to the vampire's fangs, and studied the model with a critical gaze. His big brown eyes appeared positively huge behind his even bigger glasses. Apparently satisfied with his work, he set the model on the desk. "He's not on the toilet. Nick said this is going to be the scariest costume ever. Maybe it takes a while to put on."

Carter rolled his eyes. He was a foot shorter than Angelo, and although he ate more than the other two boys combined, he never seemed to gain any weight. He also couldn't settle on a color for his short, spiky hair. This month it was dyed candy-apple red, but a few spots of last month's Day-Glo yellow still showed through above his ears. "My grandma could put on a costume faster than this and she's so old she has hieroglyphics on her driver's license."

"Not a pretty picture," Angelo said with a shudder.

Carter jumped to his feet, pressed one hand to his lower back, and shuffled across the room. "Come give your Granny Goulash a big wet smackerooni, and I'll let you have one of my stale oatmeal toffee bars. Or

is this something I scooped out of Fluffy's litter box? Can't really seem to remember."

Angelo grimaced. "Remind me never to go to your grandma's for Thanksgiving."

Before Carter could respond, an ominous voice that sounded as though it were talking through a pile of wet blankets spoke from inside the bathroom. *"Two . . . more . . . minutes."*

Angelo cocked an eyebrow and glanced toward the door. "This is gonna be good."

It was October 28, three days before Halloween, the boys' favorite holiday of the year—even better than Christmas or the Fourth of July. The candy was great, and going to haunted houses was cool too. But their favorite part was coming up with costumes that were scarier than the ones from the year before.

Carter dropped onto the chair and dug to the bottom of the chip bag. "I bet it's a mummy."

"Nope. We did mummies three years ago. Remember? You forgot to wear anything but your boxers under the bandages."

"How was I supposed to know it was going to rain?" Carter said, frowning at the memory of having to run home in nothing but his underwear and a few strands of soggy brown crepe paper. And the worst part was,

he only had half a bag of candy when the downpour hit.

In the four years since they'd discovered their mutual love for monsters and become best friends, Angelo, Carter, and Nick had gone trick-or-treating together every Halloween. One year they all went as headless horsemen, complete with bloody neck stumps and gruesome severed heads. Another year they were chain saw–wielding surgeons, with spare body parts sticking out of their lab-coat pockets.

They'd become something of a legend around their neighborhood. Every year the other kids—and even the parents—waited to see what the "Three Monsterteers," as they called themselves, would be. This year it was Nick's turn to come up with the idea, and although they knew he'd been working on the costume for months, he'd remained extremely secretive about what that costume was. But tonight, three days before Halloween, was the big unveiling.

"Do you think there are such things as *real* monsters?" Carter asked, eyeing Angelo's vampire model. "You know, actual bloodsuckers and stuff like that? Or do you think it's only in the movies?"

"Definitely not just the movies," Angelo said. "I read this story last month about three hunters who got lost in some woods way up north." He was always

searching for new stories and articles about monsters, haunted houses, aliens, or other creepy stuff he could add to his monster notebook.

"What happened to them?" Carter upended the chip bag and dumped the last of the crumbs into his mouth.

"They hiked till it started getting dark," Angelo said, rubbing his glasses on the front of his shirt. "Finally, they figured they weren't going to find their camp before morning, so they decided to light a fire. Only they just had one match. Two of them went out looking for branches and stuff while the third guy carved up a couple of sticks."

"And?" Carter asked, his voice quiet.

Angelo wiped his palms on his jeans. "When the two hunters came back from getting wood, there was a pile of kindling and a pocketknife on the ground. But the third guy was gone. They shouted like crazy, but they couldn't find him anywhere. By then it was getting really cold. They figured maybe he went to take a leak or something, so they were going to start the fire without him. Just before they lit the match, a cloud blew over the moon, and everything went dark."

"Go on, go on," Carter said, unconsciously crumpling the empty bag in his hands.

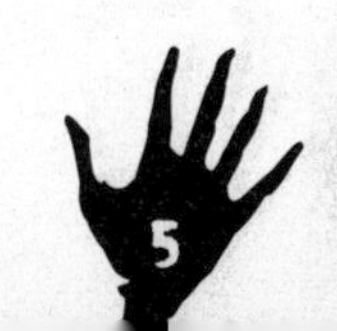

Angelo held his fingers in front of him, as though striking a match. "The guy lights the match, and he sees two pairs of eyes looking back at him. One is the second hunter's. But the other set is . . . red. Both of the guys swear they saw a hairy face, with a big, humped forehead and wicked-sharp teeth as long as their fingers. They said the creature was squatting down, and its belly was all swollen out like it just ate a huge meal. And here's the totally sick part—it was wearing the torn shirt of the third hunter across its shoulders like a trophy."

"Werewolf?" Carter breathed.

Angelo nodded knowingly. "The cops figure the only reason it didn't eat the other two guys was 'cause it filled up on their friend."

At that moment, the bathroom door creaked open a few inches and a hand reached out and shut off the bedroom light. Both boys gasped. As the door opened all the way, Carter and Angelo squinted into the bathroom, which was lit by a strange purple glow.

"Nick?" Carter's voice came out shakier than he intended. That story about the hunters had really gotten to him.

Instead of an answer, there came a wet, chuckling sound.

Something appeared in the doorway, and Carter's stomach somersaulted into his throat. The figure that stepped out of the bathroom was hunched slightly, but it still stood a full foot taller than Nick. From one side of its face, a single eye glared a baleful red. The other side was a mass of twitching muscle and shining white bone.

The creature shambled into the room, and although Carter knew it had to be Nick, he still found himself pushing back into the beanbag. The creature was dressed in the torn rags of a shirt and pants. Through the rips and holes, the gray flesh of its arms and legs appeared to be peeling away in spots. It moved with the slow, jerky steps of a puppet.

"Zombie," Angelo whispered, not sounding too steady himself.

Hearing Angelo's voice, the figure swiveled its head toward him. The zombie's mouth opened in a snaggle-toothed grin, and the creature reached into the front of its shirt and pulled something out. For a moment, Carter couldn't see what it was holding, but he could tell something was moving in its fingers. Then he realized what it was, and all the breath whooshed out of his lungs. The zombie gripped a human heart in its fist.

The heart was beating.

As though taking a bite of a fresh apple, the zombie brought the beating heart toward its lips and said, "Behold, your new costume."

"What did you think of the heart?" Nick asked. It was a sunny Friday afternoon, the day after he had shown his friends the zombie costume, and the three of them were walking home from school. They'd been discussing their Halloween plans all day long.

"Freaking awesome," Carter said. "I can't believe it actually beats."

"Did it scare you?" They stopped and waited for the light to turn green so they could cross Pleasant Hill Boulevard.

"Are you kidding?" Carter scoffed. "I totally knew it wasn't real."

Angelo looked up from the book he was reading

about extraterrestrials that harvested human organs. "So that dark stain on the front of your pants was apple juice?"

"You're full of it." Carter's face went red, and he quickly changed the subject. "I guess you made the heart out of cherry Jell-O or something, huh?"

Nick grinned at Angelo. "Actually, it's two balloons covered with toilet paper and latex, painted red. You make the heart beat by squeezing another balloon attached to the end of a rubber hose. I read about how to do it on the internet." Even he was impressed with how well it had turned out. It was sort of disgusting just holding it.

"Grossed me out," Angelo said, closing his book. "At least a little. But I don't think zombies eat hearts. I'm pretty sure they crave human *brains*."

"Who cares?" Carter pulled a slightly squashed Snickers bar out of his pocket as the light changed. "All I care about is that we get tons of candy."

"And that we scare everyone," Nick reminded him. "Remember how jealous Angie Hollingsworth was last year when we did the werewolves?" Angie and her friends Tiffany and Dana were almost as fanatic about monsters as Nick and his friends were. Every year they tried to outdo the boys' costumes. And every year

they failed. At least as far as the Three Monsterteers were concerned.

"Their Cerberus was completely unbelievable." Angelo agreed. "Whoever heard of giggling hell hounds? Speaking of werewolves, can you guys spend the night? I rented *The Beast Must Die.*"

Carter made a face. "Isn't that movie like a hundred years old? Why didn't you rent something newer like *Saw IV*?"

"My mom won't let me watch R-rated movies." Angelo shrugged. "Besides, Peter Cushing plays Dr. Lundgren. It's a classic."

"I can't," Nick said. "I've got a ton of homework." He shifted his backpack. Over the past couple of weeks, he'd been spending more time on the costumes than he had on his assignments. "If my parents find out I'm two weeks behind on math and science, they'll ground me for sure. No way I'm being stuck home on the best night of the year."

Silently, the three boys pondered how awful it would be to get grounded on Halloween, of all nights. As they turned onto Hamilton Drive, Angelo brought up a problem they'd been thinking about for the last month. "What are we going to do about Frankenstein this year?"

Frankenstein was the code name they'd given Cody Gills, the meanest kid at Pleasant Hill Elementary School. At six feet two inches tall, and weighing just over two hundred pounds, he was the biggest kid in sixth grade, and even in most of the junior high as well.

Frankenstein made it his personal goal to torment the Monsterteers every chance he got. Halloween was the worst, when he spent the entire night hunting them so he could beat them up and steal their candy. The last couple of years they'd been able to avoid him by going to different neighborhoods or ducking into houses when he came by. But that didn't mean their luck would hold up.

"What if we tell him we're going as killer surgeons again this year," Carter suggested. "That way he'll spend all night looking for kids in bloody scrubs."

Nick considered the idea briefly. "Don't you think he'd get a little suspicious when he saw three matching zombies? It's not like we fit in with the average trick-or-treaters."

Angelo nodded and kicked an empty Coke can lying in the gutter. "He's not the brightest bulb in the chandelier. But even *he's* not that dumb."

"I guess we could go to another neighborhood again," Nick said with a grimace. In movies and books, monsters were cool. But the real-life variety that beat

you up and laughed in your face when they made you cry weren't nearly as fun.

"But then we'd miss showing up Angie," Carter said around a mouthful of chocolate.

Caught up in their conversation, none of the boys had been paying attention to what was going on around them, so it wasn't until a long shadow appeared over the Coke can Angelo was kicking that they looked up and saw who was standing on the sidewalk in front of them.

"Hello, wusses," Frankenstein said, his muscular arms flexing as he cracked each of his knuckles. Even though he was only twelve, he already had a couple of long hairs sprouting from the tip of his chin, and the beginnings of sideburns.

Nick felt the spit dry up in his mouth. Had Frankenstein overheard what they were saying? If so, they were dead. "Hey, Frank—I mean, Cody."

Carter took a quick step backward, but Cody darted forward, wrapped an arm around the smaller boy's neck, and pulled him close. Dropping his half-eaten candy bar, Carter tried to twist out of the bully's grasp, but Cody held him tight.

"Planning your lame Halloween costumes again?" Cody asked with a lopsided sneer. "What's it going to be this year? Princesses? Angel-boy can be Cinderella,

Stick can be Snow White, and the midget here can be . . ." He frowned, apparently unable to think of another princess.

"Sleeping Beauty?" Carter gasped, his face going bright red as Cody continued to squeeze his neck.

"Leave him alone." Nick moved forward, his heart pounding against his ribs. He knew Cody was twice his size and could smash him to a pulp, but the sight of Carter hanging helplessly in the bully's grip flipped some kind of switch inside him.

Cody grinned. "You want to fight, Nick the Stick? Bring it on. I'll even fight you with one hand."

Nick had been hoping Cody would release Carter to take a swing at him. But the bigger boy kept his left hand clamped around Carter's neck as he made a fist with his right. Could the three of them take the bully together? Nick thought there might be a chance if they all rushed him at the same time. But Angelo was holding his book in front of him like he couldn't decide whether to stay or run. And Carter was looking more and more dazed by the second.

"What's the matter, Snow White?" Cody chortled. "Did you lose your seven dwarves?"

Nick couldn't remember later what made him do it. Maybe it was the way Carter's eyes were rolling back in his head. Maybe it was the idea of Cody trying to

ruin what was supposed to be a great Halloween. Or maybe it was just all the movies he'd seen where the hero is backed into a corner and the only way to save his friends is by ramming the stake into the vampire's heart, or shooting the werewolf with a silver bullet.

In this case, his silver bullet was Carter's candy bar, lying on the sidewalk. One minute Nick was standing there, fists clenched in anger, and the next minute he had scooped the chocolate mess off the sidewalk and smashed it in the bully's face.

What happened after that took place so quickly no one could say exactly how it occurred. Stunned by the unexpected Snickers bar offensive, Cody released Carter's neck. Either Carter made an amazingly quick recovery, or he'd been faking a little. As soon as Cody released his grip, Carter's feet hit the ground running. Apparently spurred into action by Carter's retreat, Angelo tucked his book under his arm and let his long legs carry him back down the street.

Nick might very well have stood there—frozen in place by the shock of what he'd done until Cody beat him to a pulp—if Carter hadn't come back for him. As it was, Carter was nearly too late. The pull of his friend yanking on his arm, and his voice screaming, "Run, you crazy man! Run!" shook Nick out of his trance just as Cody wiped the chocolate from his face. Nick had one quick glimpse of Cody's hate-filled, bloodshot eyes—which really did look just like Frankenstein's monster—and then he was running for his life.

Something caught at his collar, yanking him backward, and he thought he was a goner until his shirt ripped all the way down his back. Ahead of them, Angelo waved his arms, yelling, "Faster! He's right behind you!"

Beside Nick, Carter was running as fast as he could, but he was also laughing so hard, tears were squirting out of his eyes. "Can't . . . believe it," he gasped. "Chocolate . . . right . . . in the . . . face."

For his part, Nick couldn't believe what he'd done either. "He's . . . gonna kill . . . me," he puffed.

Carter nodded, holding his stomach as he ran. "Totally . . . worth . . . it."

Carter's humor was contagious. By the time they caught up with Angelo, both he and Nick were busting a gut, trying to run and laugh at the same time. Cody was twenty or thirty feet behind and losing steam fast. Frankenstein was big, but at least he wasn't quick.

"Come on," Angelo said, shaking his head as if he couldn't understand either of them. "If we cut over Dinosaur Hill, we can get back home before he gets there."

"Don't worry." Carter dropped into a slow jog. "When we run into him again, Nick can fight him off with a Twinkie."

Carter caught Nick's eyes, and the two of them burst into gales of laughter all over again.

By the time they split up to go to their own houses, all three boys were covered with dust. Dinosaur Hill Park was a great shortcut, but it was a steep climb up a dirt trail. As the adrenaline wore off, Nick's worry came back. Frankenstein would never forgive him for what he'd done, and having his Halloween candy taken might be the least of his worries.

As he walked up his lawn, the front door swung open. His first thought was that Cody had beaten him back and somehow gotten into his house. But it wasn't Frankenstein standing in the doorway. It was his mother. She had an anxious look on her face.

"Where have you been?" Mom asked, pulling him through the door. "I drove to the school looking for you."

Nick considered telling her about Frankenstein, but decided it would be better to let it go for now. "Carter, Angelo, and I cut through the park."

"Well, come inside and get cleaned up," she said. "I need you to pack a suitcase."

"A suitcase?" Nick froze in the entryway. "Why? Where are we going?"

His mother pushed him toward the bathroom. "Your great-aunt Lenore passed away last night. Look at you, you're filthy. What happened to your shirt? And what's that all over your hands?"

"Aunt who?" Nick had never heard of any Lenore.

"Lenore Braithwaite. She's your father's aunt. You haven't seen her since you were a baby. But she died last night unexpectedly, and we're flying out for the funeral."

Great-aunt? Flying? None of this made sense to Nick. But one thought suddenly rose to the top of his mind. *"When?"* he asked, panic filling his voice. "When is the funeral? And where?"

"Sunday afternoon. In a small town outside Baton Rouge, Louisiana."

"Louisiana?" Nick froze. "But Sunday's Halloween!"

Lines creased his mother's forehead. "I'm sorry." She sighed with a frown. "I really am. But I'm afraid you'll have to miss trick-or-treating this year."

By Saturday morning, Nick was hoarse from begging his parents. But none of his pleading had done a bit of good.

"Angelo's mom says I can stay with them. That way I won't have to miss school."

His mother, who was walking around the house closing blinds and checking to make sure the windows were all latched, stopped and put her hands on her hips. "I know how choked up you'd be to fall behind on your homework. Especially your *math and science*."

Nick swallowed. How had she known?

"We'll be back by Tuesday. Missing a day of classes won't kill you. I'll bet your friends would even be willing to pick up your assignments. And you can get a lot of your back work done on the plane."

Realizing that arguing with her was a lost cause, Nick walked out the front door to try his father.

"Dad," he said, handing his father a duffel bag full of shoes. "Did you ever really, really want something?"

Piling the duffel in the back of their car, between a rolling suitcase and a suit bag, his father seemed to give the question serious consideration. Finally, Nick thought, one of his parents was ready to see reason.

"Just yesterday, I really, really wanted a roast beef sandwich with brown mustard and lots of Bermuda onions. But when I checked the lunch your mom packed, it was chicken salad on raisin bread. It turned out to be almost as good as the roast beef, though. And there was a Ding Dong for dessert. So it all worked out in the end."

Nick rolled his eyes and groaned. He knew his dad was kidding him, but this wasn't a laughing matter. "Think about when you were my age. Wasn't there ever one thing you wanted so bad you knew you would die if you didn't get it?"

Dad turned and leaned against the back of the car. "I know how much this Halloween means to you," he said, folding his arms across his chest.

Nick shook his head. "If you did, you wouldn't make me go to some stupid funeral for an aunt I've never even heard of."

His father put up a hand. "Whoa there, do you really think your mother and I are making you come with us just to be mean?"

"It seems like it."

"You might not remember your great-aunt. But trust me, she remembered you. The day Lenore found out your mom was pregnant with you, she mailed out a check for a thousand dollars to help with the hospital bills. She wouldn't let us pay her back, either. Every year, on your birthday, she sent another thousand dollars to go toward your college fund."

Nick stared at his father, amazed. "Is she rich or something?"

"No. She just cared about you. She said she always felt the two of you shared a special connection. Over the years, we've sent her pictures and updates. She used to talk about coming here, and we kept promising to take you there. But now . . ." Dad chewed his lower lip. "I think it would mean a lot to her to know you came to her funeral."

Nick wanted to tell his dad how much wearing the zombie costume with his friends meant to him, but he

bit back the words and swallowed hard. "How come I've never heard of her before now?"

At first Nick didn't think his father was going to answer. He stared up into the sky. But then he nodded as though coming to a decision. "The thing is, Nick, your aunt Lenore has always been a little . . . peculiar."

"What do you mean *peculiar*?" Nick asked. "Like, crazy or something?" Why in the world would his parents want him to go to the funeral of a crazy aunt?

"Not crazy. And not peculiar in a *bad* way. It's just that Lenore was raised in a different place and time than us. Some of those small bayou towns . . . well, they look at the world a little differently than we do out here. They believe different things. Your mother and I thought it would be better if we waited until you were older before you were exposed to all that."

Nick had no idea what his dad was talking about. But it was clear he was going on the trip, whether he liked it or not.

"You know, you could always take your costume with you," Dad said. "I'm sure they go trick-or-treating in Louisiana, too."

"It wouldn't be the same," Nick said. Looking across the yard, he saw Angelo and Carter waiting for him up

the street. They looked as depressed as he felt. Leaving his dad to finish with the car, he walked to his friends.

"Any luck?" Angelo asked—his big brown eyes hopeful.

"Nah." Nick kicked the curb with the toe of his sneaker. "I have to go with them." The truth was, he felt like bawling, but he didn't want to let his friends see him cry.

"We won't go trick-or-treating without you," Carter blurted. "We'll just stay home, and . . . you know . . . watch scary movies or something."

Angelo looked at Carter like he was crazy. But then he nodded. "It wouldn't be fair to go without you. Especially since you made the costumes and everything."

"Are you kidding?" Nick glared at his friends. "You think I'm going to let all that work go to waste? It's bad enough that *I* can't go trick-or-treating. It would suck rocks if I knew you guys were sitting around on Halloween night too."

Angelo glanced at Carter and they both dropped their eyes.

"I mean it," Nick said, balling up his fists. They were his best friends in the world, but he would punch them both in the nose if they didn't quit talking like that. "Have your parents take a ton of pictures. And scare a bunch of little kids for me."

Carter grinned. "We'll scare 'em so bad they'll have nightmares for a month."

"I brought this for you to read on the plane," Angelo said, holding out a book.

Nick read the cover. "'A Brief History of Voodoo'?"

Angelo nodded. "That stuff's supposed to be big around New Orleans. It's all about voodoo dolls and voodoo queens. I think it's even got some stuff about zombies in it."

"Thanks," Nick said, taking the book. "This is awesome."

Angelo elbowed Carter. "Didn't you have something too?"

"Huh? Oh, right." Carter reached into his pocket and pulled out a bag of beef jerky. "This is for you to eat on the trip. I hear airplane food stinks."

As Nick took the bag, a piece of jerky fell out of a small opening at the top.

Carter's face went red. "Sorry, I got kind of hungry on the way over."

Just then, Nick's dad closed the back of the car, and his mother came out of the house. "Guess I better go."

"Be cool," Angelo said.

Nick started backing toward his house. "Look out for Frankenstein."

"I'll bring a couple of Three Musketeers in case we see him," Carter said, sounding choked up.

"Nah. Go with Milky Ways. They have nougat *and* caramel." Nick turned away quickly, clutching the book and the jerky. He couldn't remember feeling this horrible in his life. He hoped his friends had a great time trick-or-treating, but he knew it was going to be his worst Halloween ever.

Carter was right. The airplane food *was* terrible. His ham sandwich tasted like sliced armpit slathered with toe jam. And the in-flight movie had lots of smooching and no monsters anywhere. Not that it mattered. As soon as they rose above the clouds, his mom made him start catching up on his homework. But his mind wasn't on math. Instead, he kept thinking about what his father had said. *Your aunt Lenore has always been a little . . . peculiar.*

What did *peculiar* mean? Had she been horribly disfigured? He imagined a gray-haired old woman with an extra eye in the middle of her head, and teeth growing out of her nose. Or maybe she killed small animals and lit empty houses on fire. But he couldn't imagine his parents staying in touch with a woman who had potential serial killer traits. And he was pretty sure he'd remember a picture of an aunt with an extra eye.

Looking up from his math problems, he saw that his father was watching the movie. His mother had her eyes closed and was snoring softly. Moving carefully, so as not to wake his mom, Nick slipped his textbook into his backpack and pulled out the voodoo book Angelo had given him.

Flipping though the introduction, he saw it had been written by an anthropologist from a big university. That surprised him. Most of Angelo's books—on topics like real-life vampires, the existence of Big Foot, or true ghost stories—seemed to be written by people whose only claim to fame was that they'd seen a creature of some kind. Did that mean there really was something to this voodoo stuff? Halfway through the book was a section on Louisiana voodoo. He quickly turned to that chapter.

For the rest of the flight, Nick lost himself in stories of charms and potions, curses and favors. He read about Marie Laveau, a New Orleans voodoo queen from the 1930s. Her power was supposed to be so strong that she overthrew all the other voodoo queens in the area and was able to earn a living as an oracle, making powders that were supposed to cure illnesses or destroy a person's enemies. Some of the voodoo queens the book described helped people. But others specialized in placing curses, causing their enemies excruciating pain, and even worse.

His eyes lit up when he thought he saw the word *zombie.* But it turned out "Li Grand Zombi" was actually some kind of serpent god who helped the voodoo queens tell the future using snakes. Still, a giant serpent who could tell the future was pretty cool.

He was reading about gris-gris—amulets that could bring luck or protect the wearer from evil—when the pilot came on the intercom to say they'd be landing in a few minutes.

Nick quickly put away his book. But he couldn't stop thinking about what he'd read. Once they'd picked up their luggage and got their rental car—a boring blue sedan instead of the red Mustang convertible Nick wanted—he worked up the courage to ask his parents what he'd been wondering. "Was Aunt Lenore a voodoo queen?"

"What?" Mom turned to stare at him over the back of her seat. "Where would you get such a crazy idea?"

"Well." Nick stalled. His mom didn't always approve

of Angelo's books and it might not be such a good idea to tell her he'd been reading one of them instead of doing his math. "Dad said we never visited Aunt Lenore because she was peculiar. So I just thought that maybe . . ."

Mom turned to Dad. "You called your aunt *peculiar*?"

Dad gave Nick a thanks-for-nothing glare in the rearview mirror and shrugged his shoulders. "I didn't mean voodoo-queen peculiar. I meant throw-spilled-salt-over-your-shoulder-or-you'll-have-bad-luck peculiar. You said yourself that she had some pretty strange ideas."

"Maybe so, but I didn't tell my son his recently deceased great-aunt was 'peculiar.'" Mom looked over her shoulder. "And where did *you* hear about voodoo anyway?"

Nick gulped. "Maybe in a movie or something?"

"A *movie*." She didn't look convinced, but at least she didn't push the subject.

Grateful to be let off the hook, Nick stared out the window. Louisiana was a lot different from California. For one thing it was hotter—even at the end of October—and much more humid. Sweat began forming under his hair and down his back as soon as they stepped out of the airport. For another thing, there were a lot more trees, and they all had some strange grayish green stuff hanging from their branches.

There was water everywhere he looked. Not blue water like the lakes and ocean he was used to, but green murky stuff that looked like something the creature from the black lagoon might crawl out of. Occasionally he could see part of what appeared to be a river to his left.

"Are there alligators out there?" he asked his dad.

"Tons of them. I hear some kids even ride them to school like horses." Dad seemed cheerful to have the subject changed from Aunt Lenore. "You can eat them too. They're supposed to be delicious with a little horse-radish. You want some alligator for dinner?"

"No, thanks," Nick said. What he wanted was a hamburger and french fries.

"Or you could try a mess of crayfish. You pull off their heads and suck out the juice."

"That's disgusting." Mom wrinkled her nose. "You can have all the alligator and crayfish heads you want, buster. But if I don't get a nice juicy steak, somebody's sleeping on the couch tonight."

"Yes, Captain my Captain." Dad snapped off a quick salute with his right hand while keeping his left hand on the steering wheel.

Mom punched Dad on the shoulder. But by the way she giggled, Nick could tell she wasn't really mad.

Nick grinned. Some of his friends thought his parents were strange, joking around like a pair of kids. But he liked it. He didn't always know whether his dad was kidding or telling the truth, but it was a lot better than having parents who were serious all the time.

A few minutes later, they left the freeway and turned onto a wide street with large houses set back behind front lawns that looked almost as long as football fields. When his dad slowed the car and turned into a long, circular driveway of white gravel, Nick's eyes nearly popped out of his head.

"Here we are," Dad called out. "Home sweet home. At least for the next couple of days."

Nick didn't know exactly what he'd expected his aunt's house to look like—maybe a two-story home with bricks and stucco, like where he lived. But the house they pulled up in front of was nothing like that. It was really old, and looked like it hadn't been painted in a hundred years. And it was big, too. There were at least twenty windows on the front alone. With long strips of yellowing white paint peeling from the walls and faded green shutters, what it looked most like was a haunted house.

Mom seemed to feel the same way. She frowned at the lumpy porch that wrapped around both sides of the house and craned her neck to look up at the flat roof with what appeared to be a black metal fence around the edges. "She lived here by herself?"

"Just her as far as I know," Dad said. "It used to be the family plantation, but she was the last one alive on her side after her dad disappeared."

"Disappeared?" Nick asked, leaning forward. This was more interesting than he expected.

"Most people think a gator got him," Dad said, so seriously Nick thought he might actually be telling the truth.

Mom shook her head. "Maybe staying here isn't such a great idea. This place gives me a bad feeling."

"Are you kidding?" Dad said, parking the car in front of the porch. "This will be great. It's got . . . *character,* and it's free. It'll be like staying in our own private hotel."

A creepy hotel, Nick thought. *One of those places where the owner cuts up his guests and feeds them to a pond full of piranhas.*

Nick opened his door and a cloud of tiny black insects swarmed into the car's air-conditioned interior. One of the specks darted straight into his mouth and Nick jumped outside, coughing and spitting.

"Blech," he gagged. "What are those things?" The cloud of bugs followed him around like he was their new best friend.

"Gnats." Dad got out of the car and stretched his arms. "They don't bite . . . much."

Nick wiped his tongue with the palm of his hand. "I think I just swallowed one."

"An excellent source of protein," Dad said. "Keep

sucking them in like that, and we may not need to feed you the whole trip."

Mom didn't seem nearly as amused. She waved her hands in front of her face, trying to keep the bugs away. "Let's get inside before they eat us alive."

Dad bounded onto the porch, and the old wood groaned. He lifted a ratty brown rug and peered under it. "The realtor said he'd leave the key beneath the welcome mat, but I don't see it anywhere."

Covering her mouth with one hand, Nick's mom grasped the shaky-looking railing. "Are you sure this is safe?"

"Of course. This place has been around for over a hundred years."

Mom tried the first step and frowned. "That's what I'm afraid of."

As his parents searched for the key, Nick pulled the collar of his shirt up over his mouth and nose and began walking toward the far end of the yard. Except for the bugs and the heat and the stickiness, this was actually kind of an awesome place. Trees fifty feet high grew so close to the side of the house that some of them actually brushed up against the walls and roof. Gray strands swung slowly back and forth from their limbs—a few so long they almost touched the

ground. It was like being in the jungle.

This really would make a great haunted house, Nick thought. He could imagine ghosts swooping out of the big old trees and disappearing into the darkened second-floor windows. And what if there were monsters in the woods? Like two-headed snakes with bloated white skin and three eyes from living too close to a nearby power plant?

As he reached the edge of the yard, the ground under his feet began to get mushy, and black water squelched up around his sneakers. How cool would it be if Carter and Angelo were here—the three of them heading deep into the swamp in search of Li Grand Zombi? Carter would be snarfing peanut butter cups by the handful while Angelo read the latest research on—

A tremendous roar ripped through the trees, and Nick stumbled backward, his eyes wide. "What was that?"

It came again, filling the air like the growl of an angry lion that had somehow escaped the zoo.

"Get away from there!" A pair of arms grabbed Nick around the waist, and suddenly he was flying across the yard—his feet barely brushing the tops of the grass. He glanced over his shoulder to see his mother carrying him, her face as white as the gravel driveway.

He had no idea she was so strong. One minute he was standing on the grass at the edge of the woods and the next he was on the porch.

"Don't ever do that again!" Mom said, her hands shaking.

"Do what?" Nick asked. He squirmed out of her tight grasp. "I was just looking into the trees. What was that sound, anyway?"

Dad tried to smile, but his face was nearly as pale as Mom's. "I believe that was an alligator."

"We are not spending a single night here," Mom declared once they'd found the key under a potted plant and were inside the house. She looked dubiously around the room, as if she suspected there might be another alligator lurking beneath the afghan-covered sofa.

After all the excitement in the yard, Nick had been hoping the inside of the house would be just as cool as the outside. He was disappointed to discover it was pretty much like any other old person's house: chairs that smelled like baby powder and dried flowers, thick orange-and-green carpet that seemed to have been cho-sen specifically for its ability to hide puke, and lots of

snow globes and porcelain figures covering the shelves.

Dad ran a finger across the top of a bureau and whistled. "Some of this stuff looks like it could actually be worth something."

Mom stepped beside him—her eyes lighting up. "That couldn't be a real Chippendale, could it?"

Nick watched his parents oohing and aahing over furniture and lamps that he wouldn't have given a second glance at a garage sale. "Don't mind me," he said, rolling his eyes. "I'm just going to find somewhere I can sit and think about how much fun Angelo and Carter are probably having right now without me." When they didn't respond, he added, "I'll try not to get eaten by a hungry reptile or bitten by an extremely venomous snake."

Neither of them appeared to be listening to a word he said, so he turned and wandered away, hoping the rest of the house would be a little more interesting.

It wasn't.

Each room he stuck his head into looked the same. Musty-smelling carpet on the floors, walls covered with framed black-and-white photographs of people he didn't know, and lots more old furniture for his parents to get excited about.

What were Angelo and Carter doing right now?

Probably trying on their costumes and making plans for how to collect the most candy while avoiding Frankenstein. He walked into the kitchen, scuffing his feet across the lumpy kitchen linoleum and feeling worse than ever. The yellow refrigerator buzzed like it was full of angry hornets. He considered checking to see what was inside, but decided going through a dead woman's food was weird. Besides, he was too depressed to eat anything.

He dropped into a kitchen chair and stared at a pair of salt and pepper shakers shaped like angels with guitars. They were set on either side of a black, life-size cat statue. When his dad said Aunt Lenore was peculiar, he'd imagined something out of a horror movie. Now he wondered if Dad had just meant she had really bad taste. Who would fill her house with vomit-colored carpet and put her salt and pepper in rock-and-roll angels?

He let out a deep sigh, and the cat statue turned to look at him.

"Geez!" he yelped, scooting his chair backward so fast it nearly tipped over.

The statue blinked its green eyes.

Slowly, Nick's racing heart returned to its normal rhythm. It wasn't a statue at all. It was a real cat. He

wondered if his parents knew Aunt Lenore had a pet.

"Hey there, little guy. Or are you a girl?" Nick reached out to pet it. Before he could get close enough, the black cat leaped silently to the floor and started toward the other end of the room.

"Here kitty, kitty," he called. He wondered whether anyone had fed it since his aunt died. "Do you want some milk?"

The cat looked back at him, and he could almost swear it smiled before disappearing through a doorway at the other end of the kitchen. Nick hurried after it, and found himself in a narrow, dimly lit hallway. The cat was at the other end. As soon as it saw Nick, it reached up to scratch its claws against a white door.

"Do you want to go out?" Nick opened the door, but instead of leading outside, it opened on an even narrower set of stairs that led down to some kind of basement. Across the floor at the top of the stairs lay an old broom. The cat started toward the broom, stopped, and hissed. Its tail rose straight up and the hairs all stood on end.

Nick picked up the broom, wondering what had freaked out the cat so much. As soon as he did, the cat darted down the stairs. This was really weird. But at least it beat sitting around watching his parents look at furniture. Still holding the broom, he followed the cat down the rickety staircase. When he reached the bottom, he couldn't see the cat anywhere. In fact, he couldn't see much of anything at all.

From the dim light shining through the open door at the top of the stairs, it looked like he was in a small room. There might have been a row of shelves on the other side, but he couldn't tell for sure. The air had a strange smell to it, sort of a mix between a science experiment gone wrong and his mother's spice cabinet. This was probably some kind of pantry, where his aunt had kept her canned food.

"Where did you go?" he called, searching for the cat in the darkness. He reached toward the wall, trying to turn on a light. But instead of finding a switch, his fingers brushed against what felt like dozens of bottles. He took one from the shelf and tried to see what it was. It felt too small to be canned fruit or vegetables. His fingers went almost all the way around it.

He squinted at the jar but couldn't see what was inside. Jelly, maybe? The thought made his stomach rumble. Holding the bottle close to his face, he sniffed the lid. It smelled of metal, dust, and something kind of rotten. If it *was* jelly, it had definitely gone bad.

At the end of the shelves—right beside the stair

rail—he bumped into a thin metal chain. He tugged on the chain, and a single lightbulb illuminated the room. Nick could now see its walls were lined with shelf after shelf of colored bottles, clay pots, and boxes of all sizes. All of them had neat black handwriting on the front, but they didn't look like anything his mom kept in their pantry at home.

What is *this place?* he wondered.

Realizing he was still gripping the tiny bottle under his nose, he held it out to look at it. Inside the glass was a yellowish liquid. His first thought was that he was holding a bottle of pee. But unless his great-aunt was a lot weirder than his parents had let on, he couldn't imagine her storing urine in her basement.

He turned the bottle around to look at the label on the other side. In the small, neat handwriting in which he might have expected his aunt to write "string beans" or "raspberry preserves" were the words:

Black Mamba Venom

50 mg

Lethal dose approximately .30 mg

Time to death 30-60 minutes

Nick's eyes went from the words to the yellow liquid inside. The bottle his aunt was storing in her basement—the bottle he'd held almost right against his lips—contained one of the most lethal snake poisons in the world.

Shaking so badly he nearly dropped the bottle, Nick stuck it back on the shelf and wiped his hands on the front of his jeans. Was it really venom? Who kept snake poison in a jar? Maybe it was just a joke—a way to scare people who came snooping around. For all he knew, it was really just pickle juice inside the bottle.

His eyes scanned across a few of the nearby labels. Bat's head root. Campeche wax. White lodestone. Peace water. Coffin nails.

Coffin nails?

All at once he realized what he was looking at, and his mouth went dry. This was no joke. And that wasn't pickle juice in the jar. The containers on his aunt's shelves held the kinds of ingredients described in Angelo's book. This wasn't Aunt Lenore's pantry. It was her voodoo supplies!

"She *is* a voodoo queen," Nick whispered to himself. Did his parents suspect? Is that why they'd never let him meet Aunt Lenore?

Looking around the room at the powders and potions in jars, boxes, and pots of all sizes and shapes, a part of him wanted to get out of there as quickly as possible. Once his parents realized what Lenore really was, they might not even stay for the funeral. He might be able to get home in time to go trick-or-treating with Carter and Angelo. But another part of him knew he'd never get a chance to explore something like this again.

In one corner of the room was a wooden desk with a roll top cover. On each of its four corners there were carved owl heads that looked so real he could almost feel them watching him. Sliding the cover open, he found a neatly stacked pile of really old-looking books.

Several of them were in a language he didn't understand. But one was called *Drawing and Capturing Spirits.* Sliding into the chair in front of the desk, he opened the book and began leafing through the pages.

Some of the chapters were really creepy, like the one titled "Le Cochon Gris, The Gray Pig: Consuming

Human Flesh." Could Aunt Lenore be a cannibal? Now he definitely didn't want to go poking around in her refrigerator. A few parts were actually kind of funny, including a skeleton named Samedi that the book claimed had an insatiable sweet tooth. He was about to read a chapter called "The Feast of the Yams" when something scraped across the basement floor. Nick jumped from his chair with a yelp, dropping the book onto the desk. Sure that some tarantula or snake had escaped from its box, he backed toward the stairs. It took him a minute to notice the black shape staring at him from inside the fireplace. In his excitement over all his other discoveries, he'd completely forgotten about the cat he had followed down here in the first place.

"Hey little guy," he said. Peeking out from behind a big, black hanging pot, the cat blinked its green eyes and scraped its claws along the fireplace floor, making the sound that had scared Nick.

As he reached out to pet the cat, Nick noticed it was sitting on a black lump in the fireplace. At first he thought it might be a piece of wood or coal, but as he bent down to get a better look, he realized it was actually a book of some kind. Someone had burned it so badly that the thick leather cover was curled and completely charred. When he reached for it, the cat hissed and its black fur spiked like something in a cartoon.

"What's the matter with you?" he asked, pushing the cat aside and grabbing the book before the cat could do more than give an annoyed *mew*.

When he picked up the book, the front cover slid completely off and several of the pages crumbled to ash. Why would Aunt Lenore burn a book? She seemed to have taken such good care of everything else in the room. Any why leave the charred remains in the fireplace? The rest of the room was so organized and neat, he couldn't imagine her leaving this mess here . . . unless she had burned it shortly before she died?

Kneeling on the cold basement floor, he brushed away the ashes to see if any of the book was still readable. The pages at the front and back were either totally destroyed or else so blackened he couldn't make out anything at all. But about halfway through, he found several pages that were still partially legible.

. . . curse appears to have failed. We tried to kill him but he was too strong for us.

Cold fear played up Nick's spine like icy fingers racing along a line of piano keys. It was hard to tell with

all the smudging and smoke damage, but the words looked like the same handwriting he'd seen on his aunt's bottles and boxes. "Tried to kill him," he murmured. It sounded like his aunt had cursed some guy in an attempt to kill him. The next readable line was a few inches lower on the page.

The bokor's power is great. I can feel him trying to get back at us from beyond the grave. E has given in. The loss of . . .

The next few words were too burned to make out, and then

. . . too powerful. I have hidden the treasure where she can never get to it. The key is beyond her reach.

A treasure? What kind of treasure? Nick glanced around the room, looking for a chest or a secret door. But the only thing he saw was the cat's green eyes glaring at him.

The next two pages were completely unreadable. But the page after that looked almost untouched.

. . . such a shame about the girl. If only we had known what she was up to. But there is nothing to be done now. I can feel the King calling me at night, beckoning me. His power is so great, his undead army so strong. If I give in, he will—

"Nicholas Charles Braithwaite!"

Nick jumped up and spun around, sure his dead aunt had come back to kill him.

What he saw was nearly as terrifying. His mother was standing at the bottom of the stairs, her face white and her eyes huge and round. She looked slowly around the room, her lips pulling down into a tight pink line as her eyes took in the voodoo ingredients on the shelves. Her gaze stopped on the bottle of snake venom. "Out. Now."

"Don't you realize what this means?" Nick said. "Aunt Lenore is—"

"You heard your mother." Nick's father crossed the room and took Nick's shoulder.

"But, Dad," Nick said, trying to pull away as his father dragged him across the room. "You have to see what I found. Look at this . . ."

Nick started to show his father Aunt Lenore's journal, if that's what it was, before realizing he had somehow crushed it in his hands when his mother shouted at him—the pages he'd been reading were nothing but black smears of ash.

CHAPTER 7

YOU MAY NEED TO BREAK OUT YOUR FRENCH CAJUN DICTIONARY FOR THIS CHAPTER

"Lenore was *not* a voodoo queen." Nick's mom looked at herself in the mirror, patted her hair, and adjusted one of her earrings. It was October 31, the morning after Nick's discovery, and the day of the funeral.

"Mom," Nick said, trying to catch her eye in the mirror, "you saw what was in that room downstairs. How can you not believe your own eyes?" His parents had locked the basement door and declared the room off-limits. Clearly they were freaked out by what they'd seen. So why wouldn't they admit what it meant?

Mom turned to look at Nick with her no-more-nonsense stare. "Your father has a room filled with model airplane parts and engines. But that doesn't make him a rocket scientist, now, does it?"

"I resent that remark," Dad said from the other side of the room, where he was trying unsuccessfully to knot his tie for the fourth time.

"That's different," Nick said, unable to believe she wouldn't admit what was right in front of her. "Lots of people build models. But how many keep coffin nails and snake poison in their basement? What else would she use them for, if not voodoo?"

Mom glared at him, and Nick knew he'd pushed her too far. "I don't know what Aunt Lenore did with those . . . *things.* And frankly, I don't care. Her hobbies are her business. I refuse to speak ill of the dead. Now go get dressed for the funeral. If we're not out the door in twenty minutes, we'll be late."

"Don't you even care that she tried to kill some guy?" Nick looked to Dad for help, but his father seemed to be intentionally avoiding Nick's eyes as he undid his tie and started on it again.

"Fine!" Nick huffed as he walked back to his room. His parents could deny the truth all they wanted, but Nick had no doubt of what his aunt had been. He thought his parents knew it too.

She was a voodoo queen. She had to be. And not the good kind that helped people—making love potions and cures. She'd been the kind that cursed people. Tried to kill them.

Might there be other voodoo queens at her funeral? Nick wasn't sure if the idea was scary or exciting. It would be awesome to meet a person who practiced real voodoo. But if they'd been enemies of his great-aunt, they might like the idea of putting a curse on her relatives. And what about the army of the undead she'd written about? Was that real, or was she just nuts?

He wished he'd taken a little more time looking around her voodoo supplies. Maybe he could have found a gris-gris, an amulet to protect him against dark magic.

Knowing how his parents felt about it, Nick didn't mention voodoo the entire drive to the funeral. He tried to keep his mind on how excited Angelo and Carter would be to hear that he had a real, honest-to-goodness voodoo queen for a relative. But even that couldn't keep him from remembering that, along with being the day of his great-aunt's funeral, it was also Halloween. The first one he could remember when he wouldn't be out trick-or-treating.

Mom looked at him in the rearview mirror and seemed to read his thoughts. "You know, there's nothing that says you can't go trick-or-treating *here*. I'm sure we could find a nice neighborhood with lots of kids—as long as there are no alligators."

Nick shook his head. "No, thanks. It wouldn't be

the same without my friends. Besides, I didn't bring my zombie costume."

"Not a problem," Dad said. "There are plenty of old sheets back at Lenore's house." He opened and closed his fingers like a pair of scissors. "We could cut a hole for a mouth. Add two for eyes. And voilà, a perfect ghost."

"Holy lame." Nick groaned. "Why don't you just buy me a Barbie costume and tie me to a pole so kids can walk by and throw rocks at me?"

Dad grinned evilly. "That can be arranged too."

The funeral was held in the graveyard outside a small chapel. Nick was surprised to see at least a hundred people crowded around his aunt's casket. Had all of them known Lenore? And how many knew what she really was? Most of the people were dressed in black or dark blue, but as they entered the graveyard, a whale of a man in a bright yellow suit stepped toward them.

"You must be Lenore's nephew," he said, wrapping Nick's dad in an immense yellow bear hug. "I tell you this thing. I know that face anywhere." He spoke with a strange accent that made his words hard for Nick to understand. *That* sounded like *dat*, *thing* like *ting*, and *I* came out as *ah,* like what the doctor told you to say when you opened your mouth.

"Yes. I'm Daniel Braithwaite," Dad sputtered, trying

to squirm out of the big man's grasp.

"Coo! You look just like her." He gave Nick's mom a hug that lifted her completely off her feet.

"Who are you?" Mom squeaked, her face going red.

"Felix Mouton," the man said, lowering her to the ground. "I'm Lenore's *entrepreneur de pompes funèbres.* Her mortician."

"I didn't . . . I mean, we didn't . . . mortician?" Mom stood a few steps away, looking like she wasn't sure if she was more afraid of alligators or the big, yellow mountain of a man. Nick knew a mortician was the person in charge of a funeral. But this man didn't look like any mortician he'd ever seen.

"Mortician, pastor, and realtor," the man said. "But everyone just calls me Mazoo. I'm the one who left you the key. How did you like the house?"

Nick started to open his mouth. If this man had been inside Aunt Lenore's house, he must have seen her voodoo stuff. But his mom gave him a sharp look.

"And who's the *p'tit boug*?" he asked, engulfing Nick's hand in his giant fingers.

"I'm not a bug," Nick said.

The man roared with laughter. "Not bug, *boug. P'tit boug* means little boy."

"It's nice to meet you, Pastor Mouton," Dad said,

seeming to regain a little of his composure. "The house is . . . unusual."

"Please call me Mazoo." The man looked at Nick and winked. "It is full of surprises." He turned back to Nick's dad and asked, "Have you given any more thought to staying here? It would be a shame to have the house leave the Braithwaite family after all these years."

Mom gave a firm shake of her head. "It is a lovely house. And she has some simply marvelous furniture. But our lives are in California. We'll be flying back tomorrow morning."

The man sighed, his bushy eyebrows hunching over his eyes like a pair of angry black beetles. "Oh well, at least I tried."

Mazoo opened his bright yellow umbrella to block the sun from his eyes and began to speak. Nick looked to see if he could spot any other voodoo queens. Or anyone who looked like they'd been cursed recently. But other than a man with a very large, very hairy mole on the side of his face, no one seemed obviously cursed. The only person who appeared to notice him at all other than Mazoo was a pinch-faced woman with long gray hair and an angry expression. She glanced over her shoulder more than once with a scowl. But

Nick couldn't tell if she was looking at him or the guy with the mole.

An old woman in a flowered hat leaned over to the woman beside her and whispered, "I don't see why they buried her *here.* This cemetery is for decent people. And everyone knows perfectly well Lenore was one of *them.*"

The two women turned their heads to the left at the same time. Nick followed their gaze and found himself looking at the woman who'd been scowling at him all through the service. She glared, and the two women quickly went back to their business.

One of them, the woman had said. Nick thought he knew what they meant. They were upset that a voodoo queen was being buried in their cemetery. Was there a different cemetery for people who practiced magic? If so, why wasn't his aunt being buried there? And if they *were* talking about voodoo queens, that meant the woman they'd been looking at—the one who'd been watching him—was . . .

He risked a quick glance to his left and saw that she was staring at him again—her eyes narrowed and her thin lips pressed tightly together. A voodoo queen was staring at him, and she didn't look happy. He gulped and tried to blend into the crowd. As the minutes

dragged on, Nick tried to listen to Mazoo's words, but all he could think about was the gray-haired woman in front of them. Maybe she wasn't really a voodoo queen at all. Maybe she was just a woman whose love potion had backfired and now she was eternally grumpy. He couldn't imagine any potion strong enough to make a man fall in love with a face like that. Or maybe that was her curse. Maybe she'd been beautiful until Aunt Lenore stirred some mysterious powder into her drink.

Nick and his parents stood as the casket was lowered into the ground. A line of people came by and told them how much they had loved Lenore. Nick kept watching for the woman, but she must have left. Relief washed over him.

Once the funeral was finished, people carried out long tables and filled them with all kinds of food and desserts. For a while, Nick completely forgot about voodoo and undead armies. Instead he focused on stuffing as much good food into his mouth as he could. Piping hot slabs of sugared ham, fresh corn on the cob, pulled pork sandwiches that made his mouth water, shrimp longer than his fingers, and the *desserts*. . . .

He was finishing off a slice of strawberry-rhubarb pie with a huge scoop of homemade vanilla ice cream—wondering if he could possibly eat a slice

of blackberry crumble without throwing up—when a hand clamped onto his elbow.

"Hello, my little friend." Nick looked up to find Mazoo towering over him. "Getting enough to eat?"

Nick tried to swallow the last bite of his pie and ended up choking on it.

Mazoo gave him a firm whack on the back and the pie cleared Nick's throat. "Did you enjoy the service?" the pastor asked when Nick had stopped coughing.

"Uh, yeah." Nick looked around for his mom and dad, but his parents were nowhere in sight.

"Your aunt, she was a very special person," Mazoo said.

Nick licked his lips and nodded silently. He had a weird feeling about this guy.

"You look very much like her," the man continued. "Perhaps you have things in common as well?"

"I have to go." Nick swallowed. "My parents don't like me leaving their sight." He tried to edge away, but the man was still holding his elbow. Could this be the man Aunt Lenore had cursed? Did he want revenge?

"You explored her house," Mazoo said. It wasn't a question. "Perhaps saw things you have questions about."

Nick looked wildly around. His father was just

coming out of the church carrying a pair of chairs. “Dad!” he shouted.

The pastor’s eyes narrowed. “The owls are filled with wisdom,” he hissed.

“Hey there,” Dad called, coming over. “How about you give me a hand setting up these chairs? I’m bushed.”

Mazoo lifted his umbrella into the air, the silver tip gleaming in the sun. Holding it like a sword, he swung the sharp tip out and down.

“No!” Nick gasped, sure the man in the yellow suit was going to kill his father. But when Mazoo lifted the handle again, the only thing impaled on it was a piece of folded paper.

“I’ll have no littering on my chapel grounds.” Mazoo held the umbrella tip toward Nick. “Mind throwing that in the trash for me, *p’tit boug*?”

“Sure.” Nick pulled the paper off the umbrella and jogged toward a trash can. As he was leaning over to throw it away, the folded sheet blew open and Nick saw a single line of handwriting inside. He turned it around so he could read it.

Trust only the cat.

"Dude!" Carter sounded both surprised and happy when Nick called from his mom's cell phone that night. "How are you doing?"

"Okay. The house we're staying in is totally creepy." Nick smiled. It was great to hear his friend's voice. It seemed like it had been a week since he'd seen him last, even though it had been less than two days. He wanted to tell Carter and Angelo about Aunt Lenore's basement and the woman at the funeral, but his parents were only a few feet away eating pizza, and he knew his mom wouldn't be happy if he started talking about voodoo. Instead he asked, "How do the costumes look?" It was two hours earlier in California, and although it was dark here, his friends would just be getting ready to go trick-or-treating.

"Gertrugic!"

Angelo took the phone and said, "Carter stuffed his mouth with sloppy joe, but I'm pretty sure he said 'fantastic.'"

Nick laughed. "That sounds like Carter."

"Hang on," Angelo said, "I'll send you a picture." A moment later a chime sounded from the phone and Nick opened an image of two terrifying zombies—one tall and wearing glasses, the other shorter with bright red hair. As usual, Carter had applied too much blood to his fake wounds. But Angelo's peeling latex skin was perfect and the human hearts looked amazing.

Nick bit the inside of his cheek, trying to ignore the disappointment he felt, knowing he should be there too. "You're totally going to show up Angie and her friends."

Angelo must have heard something in Nick's voice, because there was a pause before he said, "The costumes are great. But not as great as they'd be if you were doing them."

"You won't even notice I'm not there," Nick said, knowing he was feeling sorry for himself, but unable to stop. He'd thought that calling his friends would cheer

him up, but it was doing just the opposite.

"No way," Carter said, coming back on the phone. "Angelo's right. Your plans are awesome. But they're not as good without you here to do the final touches. You're, like, a monster artist."

"Thanks." Nick swallowed.

"Are you going trick-or-treating . . . you know, out there?" Angelo asked hesitantly.

"Nah, probably just a bunch of lame little kids in superhero costumes around here. I'm going to go out on the porch and read that book you gave me."

There was a long pause before Carter said, "That's it. We're staying in too. It's not right going without you. I can steal my sister's candy when she gets back."

"Not a chance. I'll see you guys Tuesday morning and I want to hear about every little kid you scared." Nick wiped the back of his hand across his eyes. "I gotta go."

"See you soon," Angelo said, his voice somber.

"I'll save you all my best candy," Carter said.

Nick knew the odds of Carter saving candy were about as good as the odds of Angie admitting the Three Monsterteers had better costumes than her and her friends. But he said, "Sounds good," and hung up the phone.

He was glad his friends would have fun, but it was going to be a horrible night for him.

"Sure you don't want to go out tonight?" Dad asked as he chewed his sixth slice of pizza and washed it down with a slug of cold root beer. "We still have time to run by a store and get a mask or something."

"No, thanks." Nick sighed, handing his mom the phone.

Dad slumped in his chair, and Nick knew he felt bad about ruining the holiday. But not nearly as bad as Nick felt. It was twelve months until next Halloween. And by then he and his friends would be some other creature. He'd never have a chance to show off the zombie costume he'd worked so hard on.

"Do you think I could maybe look around Aunt Lenore's basement for just a few minutes if I promise not to touch anything?" he asked. It was the only thing he could think of that might take his mind off of his troubles. Besides, he also wanted to see if he could find anything else about those mysterious notes in the burned book.

Dad swallowed his last bite of pizza and opened his mouth, but Mom spoke first. "Absolutely not. Some of that stuff is poisonous."

"It's not like I'm going to start randomly putting things in my mouth."

"Your mom's right," Dad said. "It's not safe. I'm going to make sure that whoever cleans the house throws all of that stuff away."

Nick bit his tongue to keep himself from saying something that would get him sent straight to bed. First they ruined his Halloween, then they wouldn't let him look at the only interesting thing on this entire trip.

"By the way, what were Pastor Mazoo and you talking about after the funeral?" Dad asked, eyeing the last two slices of pizza in the box.

Maybe it was because he was upset at his parents for not trusting him, or maybe it was because he didn't know for sure exactly what Mazoo had been talking about, but Nick wasn't ready to tell his mom and dad what the pastor had said to him. He just had a feeling that if he mentioned the weird conversation they'd had, his parents would be even more concerned than they already were. "Nothing really. He asked me if I liked the service." At least that part was true. He sighed again and rested his chin in his hands.

"If you're going to sit around and mope, I'm sure I can find you some more homework to finish," Mom said.

"Fine." Nick grabbed the voodoo book out of his backpack—not caring if his parents saw it or not—and carried it out the front door to sit on the porch.

"Stay away from the woods," his mother called as the screen door banged shut.

"Like you care," Nick said, making sure to keep his voice low enough that his parents couldn't hear him. Outside, the sun had set completely and a full moon was rising above the horizon. Nick fished the piece of paper from the cemetery out of his pocket and studied it for what felt like the hundredth time that day. The moon gave off plenty of silver light to read.

Trust only the cat. What was that supposed to mean? How exactly were you supposed to trust a cat? It wasn't like the cat had a lot to say. In fact, he hadn't seen the cat since they came back from the funeral.

Maybe it wasn't even a message. It could be some guy was just writing a note to himself, like, *Remember to pick up orange juice.* Although he couldn't imagine what kind of person would remind himself to trust a cat. Even if it *was* a message, that didn't mean it was for him. It didn't have his name on it or anything. It had just been blowing across the ground. Anyone could have picked it up, and anyone could have dropped it.

Besides, he was going home in the morning. So it didn't matter whether he trusted the cat or not. Still, he had a nagging feeling that there was more going on with his aunt than he or his parents knew. As good as it

would be to get back home, a part of him wished he had a little more time to snoop around, especially without his parents looking over his shoulder all the time.

He stuck the note in his pocket and opened the voodoo book, hoping it might have some clues he'd missed before. He tried to pay attention to what he was reading, but it had been a long day and soon his head started to nod. The words swam on the page. His eyes slid closed as the book dropped onto his lap and he began to dream.

In his dream, he was standing at the edge of a shadowy green swamp. A black cat emerged from the trees and rubbed itself against his legs. "Hello, Nick," the cat said, swishing its long tail.

"Who are you?" Nick asked. In real life he'd have been shocked speechless that a cat could talk. But in his dream it seemed perfectly natural. He was more surprised that the cat knew his name.

"I'm a . . . friend of the family," the cat said.

Nick rubbed sweat off his face. He couldn't ever remember sweating in a dream before.

"Was my aunt a voodoo queen?"

"Oh, yes-s-s-s," the cat hissed. And now it was no longer a cat at all, but a snake. "Lenore was one of the most powerful voodoo queens."

Although sweat still beaded on his arms and face, Nick began to feel cold inside. "She never hurt anyone, did she? She didn't put a curse on them or . . ."

"Did she ever hurt anyone?" the snake asked, wrapping itself around his ankles. "Why, that's what voodoo queens do. They wrap themselves around you with their powders and their spells, their dolls, and their ceremonies." Around and around the snake coiled, moving up his body. "They squeeze you until they get exactly what they want."

Nick tried to scream, but the snake crushed his lungs so he couldn't draw in air. All at once, he remembered the gris-gris. He needed an amulet of protection. He raised his hands to his neck, but there was nothing there. The snake opened its mouth wider than he could have imagined, as if it was going to swallow him whole.

"Help!" he tried to scream. "Someone help me!"

Nick woke up and something was touching his face. "Ahh!" he yelled, sure he was about to be eaten by a giant snake. But it was only the cat.

"Man," Nick said, trying to catch his breath. "You scared the heck out of me." Purring, the cat curled into his lap and let Nick pet it. The dream had seemed so real, but now that he was awake, he had a hard time remembering exactly what it had been about. "Where have you

been hiding all day?" he asked, rubbing the cat's silky fur.

"Meow," the cat said, as if trying to answer him. It gave one last rub against his chest before jumping to the porch and hopping from stair to stair until it was standing on the grass. Nick expected the cat to run off, but it turned to look at him and meowed again.

"You want me to come with you?" He felt silly talking to a cat, but no one was around to see him, and somehow it felt right—as if the cat could actually understand what he was saying.

"Meow." The cat turned and trotted toward the side of the house. Nick looked through the window behind him. The downstairs lights were all off and the upstairs bedroom light, where his parents slept, was on. They must be reading. He wouldn't go anywhere near the woods, of course, but he wanted to see where the cat was going.

As Nick walked down the stairs, the cat turned its head to look at him before disappearing around the corner of the house. "Wait up," Nick called, breaking into a jog.

Reaching the corner of the house, he saw that the cat was headed toward the backyard. It didn't bother slowing down for him, as though confident he was following now.

Where was the cat leading him? Back to the basement? He'd promised his parents he wouldn't go in there. And whether he wanted to admit it or not, they were probably right. Who knew what all the stuff in those bottles would do? Just breathing in the wrong thing might cause consequences he couldn't imagine.

The cat didn't head for the house, though. It hurried across the backyard at a pace that made Nick have to run to keep up. When it reached the far edge of the lawn, where the overgrown grass met the woods, it glanced at Nick before slipping into the trees.

"Hey!" he called racing after it. "Don't go in there. You'll barely be an appetizer for an alligator."

When he reached the spot where the cat had disappeared, he saw it about ten feet into the woods. "Get out of there," he called, keeping an eye out for anything moving.

The cat ran a few feet farther, turned, and meowed. *Come with me,* he could almost hear it saying.

But he couldn't. Not with alligators and snakes and who knew what else slithering around in there. And especially not at night.

"Meow." The cat paced back and forth, its eyes glowing in the darkness.

Nick studied the woods. There was something unusual about the spot where the cat kept pacing.

He couldn't put his finger on it exactly. To either side the ground was swampy and damp, but where the cat stood meowing at him, it looked dry. And while most of the ground was covered in ferns, bushes, and trees, this area was surprisingly free of plants. It was almost as if someone had cleared it out on purpose. As if it was a . . .

"A path," he whispered. Now that he was looking for it, he could easily see someone had cleared a path through the trees. But who, and to where?

Trust only the cat, the note had said. Is this what it was talking about? Did someone want him to follow the cat on this path in the woods? Did they think he should see where it led?

He looked up at the light shining in his parents' bedroom. They'd freak if they discovered he was gone. Besides, he'd heard that alligator for himself. It would be crazy to go in there.

But this would probably be his only chance. He knew his parents were going to sell the house, and they were leaving in the morning. If he didn't follow the path now, he'd never know what lay at the end of it. Didn't he deserve some fun after giving up his Halloween?

He looked down at the dirt and spotted a pair of shoe prints leading away from the house. They were slightly smaller than his feet and smooth on the bottom.

The kind of footprints an old woman might make if she were wearing slippers. That was what finally decided him. If his aunt Lenore had made this path, how dangerous could it be?

"Okay," he said, taking a deep breath. "Lead on, cat. Let's see where this goes."

Nick stepped from the grass onto the path and paused. The trees that had looked spooky but cool in the daytime now only looked spooky. Their gnarled trunks gazed down on him like disapproving old men's faces—angry that he was trespassing. Their hanging moss looked like beards.

"Trust the cat," he said to himself. "There's nothing to be scared of." He listened for the roar of an alligator, but all he heard were frogs and insects, so he continued on. "Cats have great night vision. If he sees something dangerous out there, he'll turn back."

It sounded good, but as the branches blocked out the moon's light—leaving him in a tunnel of almost complete darkness—his heart began to pound. In the movies, when the main character headed into the woods, it was exciting. You leaned toward the screen, eager to see what would happen next. Real life was nothing like that. Every time he heard a cracking branch or something slithering through the mud, he froze, sure he was about to become some creature's meal.

The cat appeared to have no such worries. It hurried along the trail at a brisk pace, meowing when Nick began to fall behind. Nick learned to watch exactly where the cat went, stepping only where it stepped. Once he veered too far to the left, and his foot slipped into black sucking mud that nearly pulled his shoe from his foot. Another time, he splashed into a pool of murky water and something splashed back in the distance.

Sometimes the trail was clear, and other times it was so overgrown he could only tell he was still on it by the fact that the cat was there. What if the cat disappeared? Could he find his way home alone? He stopped still at the thought, wondering if he should turn back now. What had seemed like an adventure before was starting to seem like a really bad idea. He'd seen the headlines—"Boy Lost in Woods." Was he going to be one of those headlines? Would he ever see his parents again?

He was about to turn around, despite the cat's impatient meowing, when something flickered through the woods ahead of him. What was that? It came again—a faint glint of silver appearing momentarily ahead and to his left, before disappearing just as quickly back into the trees. He leaned forward, hands balled into fists at his sides. "Who's there?"

Nothing answered.

"Meow." The cat stood on its back feet and waved both front paws in the air. The insects, which had paused their chirping and buzzing at the sound of Nick's voice, started up their night music again.

"Okay," Nick said. "But only a few more minutes. If we haven't found what you want to show me by then, I'm going back."

Silently the cat turned and hurried ahead. Nick followed, hoping he wasn't making a big mistake. A minute later, the trail seemed to end at a slow-flowing stream six feet or so across. "That's it?" Nick asked. "You brought me all this way to show me a stinky creek?"

Flicking its tail, the cat bunched its small body and leaped directly at the water. Nick watched, amazed, and waited for the cat to splash in the creek and come bounding back—a wet angry mess. Instead the cat seemed to bounce across the water like a skipping

stone, rising and falling until it reached the far bank.

"How the heck did you do that?" Nick approached the stream. In the glow of what little moonlight could make it through the tree branches overhead, he spotted a flat rock rising just above the surface of the water. Then another, and another. Stepping-stones leading across the stream. "Nice," he said, nodding his head in approval. Whoever made this trail had gone to a lot of trouble to do it right.

Holding his hands out for balance, he jumped from rock to rock until he reached the other side. As soon as he was across, he spotted a metal gate, rusty and pitted with age. The cat must have gone through the bars of the gate, because it was nowhere to be seen. Nick placed a hand on the cold iron framework and pushed. The gate swung open with a high-pitched *rrrreeeeeeee.* A low mist that hadn't been there on the other side of the gate floated around his legs as he stepped through. Walking between a pair of high bushes, he saw someone looking back at him through the mist.

"Hello?" he called. The figure didn't respond. "Who's there?" Nick took another step forward, his legs trembling. The face was looking right at him, but it didn't speak or move.

"Who are you?" Nick said, trying to sound brave. "What are you doing behind Aunt Lenore's house?" He

took another hesitant step before realizing why the figure wasn't moving. It was a stone statue. A statue of an angel. Looking around, he could see there were more of them as well. And that wasn't all. Dozens of stone platforms rose out of the mist. What was this place?

Fifty feet or so to his right he saw what looked like a small stone building. With no trees to block it here, the moon hung big and round in the sky. It was full—a werewolf moon, Angelo would have called it. Its light turned the fog an eerie silver. Nick reached the building, but he still didn't know what it was. Two steps led up to a door with a pillar on each side. There was something carved into the stone above the door. It was partially covered with dirt and moss. Nick climbed the steps and rubbed the dirt away with the palm of his hand.

BRAITHWA

As the last of the dirt fell away, he realized what it said. Braithwaite. His last name. At the same time he understood what this building was—where *he* was. He tried to step backward, forgetting the step behind him, and fell onto the soggy ground. His breath whistled in and out as if his throat had shrunk to the size of a straw.

The path he'd followed had led him to a cemetery. The angels and platforms were graves—raised above the ground to keep them above the waterline. And this

building poking out of the mist above him was a crypt. A house for the dead. For *his* dead.

Something squelched in the ground behind him, and Nick leaped to his feet. "Who's out there?" he called, trying to see through the fog. Thunder crashed in the clear night sky, and a cold wind whipped through the graveyard, making the mist look like dancing ghosts.

What sounded like footsteps came from his left, and Nick spun around, nearly falling again.

"It is time," a voice whispered out of the darkness.

Nick gasped. What did the voice mean? Time for what? He looked at his watch. 11:59 and fifty seconds. Ten seconds until midnight on Halloween night. With a full moon overhead. Nine seconds, eight, seven, six. What would happen at midnight? He wanted to run out of the cemetery, but the mist had risen so high he couldn't tell which way was which.

Five, four, three. The ground began to glow green under his feet. The green spread from the ground up through the fog. It touched stone and began to race from tomb to tomb like a spreading cancer. Nick's breath came fast and sharp. It had to be the old woman out there. The voodoo queen. She'd tricked him into coming here, and now she was going to kill him.

Two, one. The time on his watch changed from

11:59 to 12:00. It was midnight.

"No!" Nick yelled. He looked around wildly, wondering which way the attack would come from. Someone pushed him in the back, and he fell toward the Braithwaite crypt. As he stumbled forward, the door swung open with a crack like the sound of a mountain tearing itself in two. Plumes of dust spun out of the doorway like miniature tornadoes. Deep inside the pitch-black stone mausoleum, something glimmered.

Nick stared into the darkness, sure he would see a dead body. Instead, on a white stone pedestal inside lay a glimmering red stone. Nick took a step forward and saw that it looked like a necklace of some kind. A red stone, like a glowing eye in a gold setting attached to a thin gold chain.

A gris-gris, his brain cried. A protection from dark magic. He ran up the stairs into the crypt. At the entrance something seemed to hold him back for a split second. Then he was through. The stone flared in his hand as he closed his fingers around it, then blinked out.

Behind him the door of the crypt slammed closed. "Help!" Nick screamed, trapped in the dark. He slammed his fists against the stone door, but it wouldn't budge. "Let me out!"

The air in the crypt seemed to be thickening. It

was hard to breathe. “Someone open the door.” He felt dizzy, as if he had inhaled some kind of poison gas. “Please . . .” he gasped. “Open . . . the . . .”

At the last moment he could have sworn he heard someone laughing.

Then he passed out.

"Come on, sleepyhead. Rise and shine."

Nick peeled his eyes open, wondering for a moment where he was. He turned his head to see his mother standing in the doorway with her hands on her hips.

"I thought you were so excited to leave," she said, cocking her head.

"I am." Nick's voice sounded scratchy, like he was coming down with a cold, and his head felt achy. Just his luck to get sick when it was time to go home. Why couldn't he have gotten sick *before* the trip and missed it completely?

He started to push himself out of bed before seeing his filthy sheets and remembering what had happened the night before. At least, he sort of remembered. He'd followed the cat to the cemetery. There'd been some sort of storm, and then . . .

He couldn't recall what had happened after that. Or how he'd gotten back. There was something about a stone building. The rest was all a blur. Could he have hit his head? Or was he sicker than he thought?

Mom sniffed. "Take a shower, too. You smell like you've been bathing in swamp water."

She waited in the hallway, and Nick waved her away. "Close the door. I'm not decent."

"Fine, Mr. Modesty. But if you're not downstairs in twenty minutes, showered and dressed, I'll drag you downstairs myself. I want to be ready to go before the movers get here."

As soon as she shut the door, Nick jumped out of bed and threw back the blankets. His sheets were covered with dirt and smeared with mud. There were several large clods, and even a worm wriggling sluggishly on the white cotton. What had he done, gone straight from the woods into his bed without cleaning off at all?

He sniffed his armpits to see what smell his mom was talking about, but he seemed to be congested too. He could barely smell a thing. He pulled the blankets off the bed—at least they were more or less dirt-free—and

shook out the sheets before realizing it was a lost cause. He'd have to sneak them into the washing machine before they left, and hope his mother didn't notice.

He stumbled into the bathroom and looked in the mirror. His skin was pale, and there were circles under his eyes. He peeled off his T-shirt and stared at his reflection. Where had *that* come from? His fingers gripped the gold chain around his neck and followed it to a red gem that looked way too big to be real. Touching the necklace brought back a memory. Someone had been there in the cemetery with him. They'd shoved him into a crypt and locked the door.

Had they tried to kill him? Had the amulet saved his life? Could it be a real gris-gris? If so, the voodoo queen who had attacked him might still be around. She might come for him again. Or his parents. Quickly he stepped into the shower. He started to take off the amulet, but if there was a dark magic user after him and his family, maybe it was better to keep it on.

He stayed under the hot water just long enough to wash away the worst of the mud and dirt from the night before, then toweled himself off and dressed in a rush. He raced down the hall, and was relieved to see his parents packing the last of their clothes into their suitcases.

"What time did you go to bed last night?" his dad asked, looking Nick up and down. "No offense, but you look like you were attacked by a mountain lion, dragged through the dirt, and then slobbered on for good measure."

Mom smacked him. "That's gross."

"I'm not really sure," Nick said, telling the truth. He had no idea when he'd come home. Or how. "Was everything okay last night?"

Mom looked up from shoving the last pair of shoes into a duffel bag. "*Okay?* What do you mean?"

Nick realized he couldn't say what he was thinking without giving himself away. "It's just that it was Halloween. Sometimes things . . . you know."

"Oh." Dad's face tightened. "You mean the voodoo queen that attacked us while we were sleeping. All Hallows' Eve and a full moon. We never had a chance."

Nick's eyes widened. His stomach felt like a ball of ice. So it *had* happened. How much of it was his fault?

"She sucked our brains out through a straw." Dad held his arms straight before him. "And made us join her legions of the living dead." He was joking. Nick let out a sigh.

Mom poked Dad in the back. "You are such a dweeb." She rolled her eyes and turned to Nick. "If you mean

sleeping on a lumpy mattress and listening to your father snore like a dump truck stuck in second gear, yes, everything was okay last night. Why? Was everything okay with you? I fell asleep reading and didn't hear you come in. You didn't go down to the basement, did you?"

"No." Nick's hand went unconsciously to the amulet under his shirt. "I think I might have fallen asleep on the front porch swing."

"I hope you didn't come down with anything. You look a little pale," Mom said. "Why don't you go downstairs and have some breakfast while I get you packed up? I made bacon and eggs, and there might be a doughnut or two left if your dad hasn't eaten them all. But move it, because I want to leave as soon as the movers come to pack up the furniture we're keeping."

"That sounds good," he said, relieved to be getting away without any closer questioning. "I'll just clear off my bed and put the sheets in the washer."

"That would be nice." Mom smiled.

Nick tossed his balled-up sheets in the washing machine, careful to turn them so most of the mud was on the inside, and went to the kitchen where there was an open box of doughnuts on the table. Chocolate old-fashioned—his favorite. Almost half the box was gone.

Clearly his dad had gotten there first.

Nick grabbed a doughnut and took a bite as he walked to the counter to pour himself a glass of juice. As soon as the food hit his tongue, he gagged and spit it into the sink.

"Something wrong?" his dad asked, stepping into the kitchen.

Nick held out his doughnut and turned it over. "I think this is spoiled or something. It tastes disgusting."

"Really?" Dad sniffed at the box and shook his head. "Mine were great." He took another one out of the box and offered it to Nick. "Here, try this one."

"No, thanks." Nick threw his doughnut in the trash and rinsed his mouth out with water. Just the thought of another bite of the sweet chocolate and cake made him want to gag.

Dad tossed his doughnut into the air, caught it on one finger, and took a bite. "Guess I could force myself to eat another one."

Nick looked at the carton of orange juice and realized that didn't sound good either. What was wrong with him? Cautiously, he picked up a piece of bacon and sniffed at it. He tried a bite. It wasn't as bad as the doughnut, but it still tasted wrong. The strangest thing was that the uncooked bacon in the package on

the counter actually sounded kind of good. That was disgusting. Maybe he really *was* coming down with something.

Nick kept an eye out for anything unusual as they packed up the car. Except for his memories, everything was as peaceful as could be. Only *he* knew that behind his aunt's house was a graveyard, and possibly something much worse.

Soon—to Nick's great relief—they were in the car and on their way, leaving behind whatever had or hadn't happened the night before. Nick considered taking off his amulet, but decided he'd leave it on, just to be safe. Halfway to the airport his mom looked over the seat at him and sniffed. "I thought I told you to take a shower."

"I did," he said, crossing a finger over his heart. "Promise."

She turned up the air conditioner. "Well, either you didn't do a very good job or you stepped in something, because you are one stinky kid."

Nick shrugged.

The flight back was mostly uneventful. At the security checkpoint, he'd started to take off the amulet before deciding it might be a good idea to leave it on

just a little longer. Surprisingly, it didn't set off the metal detector.

Mom insisted his dad sit between her and Nick. Dad, who was suffering from allergies, didn't mind because he couldn't smell a thing. Just before they closed the doors, as the last passengers were storing their suitcases, Nick had the odd feeling someone was watching him. When he turned around, though, the only person he saw was a cranky flight attendant telling people to turn off their cell phones and MP3 players.

A couple of hours later, lunch was served. Nick tried a bite of his cold turkey sandwich. The bread tasted like sawdust, but he managed to choke down a few bites of the meat after peeling it off and eating the turkey by itself.

Mom stared over at him and frowned. "Are you feeling okay?" she asked.

"I guess." He wasn't achy or anything, and he hadn't been coughing, but he did feel a little off.

She reached over and put the back of her hand against his forehead. "You don't feel feverish," she said with a frown. "In fact, if anything, you feel a little too cool."

Dad punched him lightly on the shoulder. "Nothing that sleeping in his own bed and seeing his friends

again won't fix. Get him home, and he'll be good as new in no time."

Nick couldn't agree more. He'd be happy to put as much distance between himself and Great-aunt Lenore's house as he could. And he wouldn't mind if he never heard about voodoo again.

The next morning, Nick was up before his alarm went off. In fact, he wasn't actually sure he'd slept at all. He must have dozed off without realizing it though, because he didn't feel a bit tired. His voice was still a little croaky, but his headache was almost gone, and his appetite was back with a vengeance. He felt like he could eat a horse, and possibly a goat, a pig, and a duck on the side.

Climbing out of bed, he stumbled a little. His right foot felt sort of tingly—like it had fallen asleep. But he was home, and today he'd be back at school with his friends. That was what mattered. Excited to hear how the zombie costumes had gone over, he hurried to the bathroom and got undressed. The amulet was still hanging from his neck. He hadn't felt like taking it off before he went to bed. Now, as he reached for it, he felt the same reluctance to remove it.

"Gris-gris," he whispered. Protection. A kind of good-luck charm. Of course he couldn't wear it forever, but for now it felt kind of good where it was. Sort of like it belonged there. Maybe he'd show it to Carter and Angelo and see their eyes widen as he explained what it was. Imagining their faces when he told them about the cemetery behind his great-aunt's house, he turned on the shower and began washing his hair.

Taking extra time to get all the swamp smell out of his skin and hair, he was nearly done before he realized he'd left the water on cold. He should have been freezing under the icy spray but it felt fine on his skin, so he left it that way. Maybe he was toughening up. After he dried off, he took a minute to sniff himself. He didn't think he smelled bad, but just to be on the safe side he used extra deodorant.

"I'm starving," he said as he came into the kitchen.

"Lucky for you," Mom said from where she was standing at the stove. "In honor of our return home, I made your favorite. Pecan pancakes and scrambled eggs."

His stomach rumbled at the thought of his mom's fluffy pancakes slathered with lots of butter and drowned in maple syrup. "One hot stack coming up," Mom said, sliding his plate across the table.

"What about me?" Dad asked as he strolled into the kitchen.

"I thought that after seven doughnuts yesterday, you'd be more in the mood for something a little lighter. Like, say, a diet granola bar," Mom said with a smile.

Dad kissed her on the cheek and began grabbing pancakes. "That's what I like about you, your wonderful sense of humor."

Nick grinned. It was good to be home. He buttered and syruped his pancakes, cut them into squares, and got ready to dig in. But as he started to put the first bite into his mouth, something felt wrong. He lifted the food to his nose and sniffed. He thought it smelled okay, but something was . . . strange.

"Everything okay?" Dad asked, sitting down at the computer and browsing the internet.

"I think so," Nick said. He lifted the bite to his mouth, stuck out his tongue, and licked a drop of maple syrup. His stomach clenched as if he'd just swallowed a mouthful of poison.

"What is it?" Mom asked, watching him closely. "Did I overcook the eggs?"

"No." Nick shook his head. The food was fine. But something was wrong with him. Why was it that his favorite foods suddenly made him feel like he was going to puke?

He was saved from answering as the kitchen door flew open and Angelo and Carter came piling through.

"You should have seen all the candy we got," Carter chirped. "I ate so much I woke up in the middle of the night and threw up."

"Excellent," Nick said, grinning.

"And the costumes were the best," Angelo added. "You should have seen Angie's face when she saw the beating hearts. She totally knew we'd outclassed them again."

"What did they go as?" Nick asked.

"Vampire cheerleaders," Angelo said. "They were pretty realistic-looking, too."

"Don't forget your field trip to the pool today," Mom reminded Nick, holding out his swimsuit.

"Right." He shoved it in his backpack and the three boys headed out the door. In all the excitement of Halloween talk, Nick didn't have a chance to tell them what had happened to him. They were almost to the school when Carter looked around nervously. "Um, you might want to try and avoid Frankenstein for the next few days."

"Why, what happened?" Nick asked, wondering what the bully had been up to this time. "Did he chase you guys while you were trick-or-treating?"

"Uh, not exactly," Angelo said. "It turns out his mom forgot to get him a costume until the last minute. The only things left in the store big enough to fit him were a snowman and Barney the Dinosaur. His mom thought a dinosaur would be scarier."

"He didn't wear it, did he?" Nick asked, covering his mouth to hold back the laughter.

"No." Angelo shot a look at Carter, who ducked his head. "He was so embarrassed he begged Carter to come up with something. He promised if we gave him a real costume he'd leave us alone that night."

Nick looked from Carter to Angelo. "So? What did you do?"

Carter bit his lip. "I suggested the crepe-paper mummy."

Nick snickered. "And it rained?"

"No," Angelo said as they entered the front of the school. "But he was waiting in the Dashners' yard to steal candy from some little kids when old Mr. Dashner turned on his sprinklers."

"Don't tell me," Nick said, laughing so hard his jaw ached. "The crepe paper dissolved and he ran home in nothing but his boxers?"

Carter shook his head and grinned. "He forgot to wear boxers. Mr. Dashner chased him halfway up the block yelling that he was going to have him arrested for indecent exposure."

Nick was still laughing at 10:30 when his teacher, Ms. Schoepf, herded them out the door to the school bus that would take them to the pool. Unfortunately, all three sixth-grade classes would be there at the same time.

"This could be bad," Carter said, pulling on his swimsuit and hurrying out of the locker room before Frankenstein showed up. With the bully on the warpath and all three of the classes in the pool at once, it was only a question of who he'd catch first.

"Maybe if we stick together we can hold him off," Angelo suggested as they waited for the lifeguard's signal to jump in.

"No way," Carter said. "He'd just drown us all. If we split up, we'll have a better chance of escaping him."

Nick dropped his towel by the edge of the pool and Carter's eyes opened wide. "Wow, what is that?"

Nick looked down, having completely forgotten he was still wearing the amulet. "Oh, uh," he stammered, a little embarrassed. "I, uh, got it at my great-aunt's house."

"It's a *necklace*?" Carter asked, raising his eyebrows.

"No!" Nick said at once. "It's more like a good-luck charm."

Angelo leaned forward to study it more closely. "I think I saw something like that in a book once." He reached toward the amulet and Nick jerked backward.

"I wasn't going to take it," Angelo said.

"I know." Nick touched his hand to the stone. It felt warm against his fingers. Why had he pulled away like that? It was almost like the amulet made him do it. Like it didn't want to be touched by anyone but him. Of course that was crazy.

"Where did you say you got it?" Angelo asked with a frown.

Before Nick could answer, the lifeguard blew his whistle. "Everybody in the water!"

Cody Gills, aka Frankenstein, came out of the locker room at that moment wearing a leopard-print bathing suit at least two sizes too small. Nick was hoping he might not notice them. But as soon as Frankenstein came out, he scanned the pool and made a beeline for the three of them.

"Good luck!" Carter yelled, diving into the pool and stroking for the other side.

"You want me to cover your back?" Angelo asked.

Nick shook his head. "Carter's right. Our best chance is to split up and confuse him."

The two of them dived into the water in opposite directions. Keeping underwater to remain hidden, Nick held his breath and stroked as hard as he could. He dodged between boys and girls, changing directions randomly to throw off any pursuit that might be headed his way. Not until he'd covered nearly three quarters of the pool did he dare to surface and look around.

As soon as he raised his head above water, he checked for his friends. Carter was at the other end of the pool hiding behind a teacher and an especially tall girl. It took Nick a couple of seconds to spot Angelo near the high dive. When he did, his friend was waving wildly in his direction and shouting something. Nick spun around, but it was too late. Cody was right on top of him.

"Nice necklace, wimp." The bully grabbed Nick's neck and before he could take a breath yanked his head under the water.

Nick tried to force Frankenstein's hands off of him, but the bigger boy's muscles were like steel. He knew the bully wanted to see him swallow water, then he'd let him up, coughing and choking, while his jerk friends laughed.

Nick closed his eyes and clamped his jaws shut. He wouldn't give Frankenstein the satisfaction of seeing him half drowned. Instead, he concentrated on holding his breath as long as he could. It wasn't nearly as hard as he thought it would be. He hadn't had a chance to fill his lungs before he was shoved underwater. His chest should be burning by now. And yet he felt no pain or discomfort. In fact, he felt really good. The water was comfortable against his skin, the outside noises muted. He floated weightless in the water.

He didn't realize Frankenstein was no longer holding him under until a strong pair of hands grabbed him and lifted him up. Nick opened his eyes and looked around. All of the kids in the pool and all of the teachers were staring at him in silence.

"Are you okay?" asked the lifeguard, clearly unnerved.

"Yeah, why?" Nick asked. Why was everyone staring at him?

The lifeguard shook his head as if he couldn't believe his eyes. "I've never seen anyone hold their breath that long."

"Come on, tell us how you did it," Carter begged, slinging his backpack toward Angelo's bunk bed and missing by a good two feet.

"There's nothing to tell," Nick said to his two friends as they hung out in Angelo's bedroom after school. "I just held my breath."

"Are you kidding me?" Carter waved his hands as he paced around. "For ten minutes? That's got to be some kind of world record or something."

Angelo went to his bookshelf, pulled out a thick paperback, and flipped quickly through its pages. "Not even close. It says here some guy broke nineteen minutes."

"Still," Carter said, plopping onto the bottom bunk

and fiddling with a video game controller. "*Ten minutes!* I start to get lightheaded after holding my breath for thirty seconds while I rinse the shampoo out of my hair. What did you do, hide one of those oxygen canisters in your mouth? Tell us how you did it. I promise we won't reveal your secret."

Nick shrugged. He had no idea how he'd done it. The lifeguard said he should consider joining the swim team. But the truth was, up until today he couldn't remember holding his breath for more than a minute or so. "I swear I don't have a clue. I've felt kind of weird ever since I went into that crypt."

"Crypt?" Angelo slammed his book closed, his eyes two big brown circles behind his glasses.

"Crypt?" Carter sprang off the bed, thunked his head against the top bunk, and collapsed at Nick's feet. "You went into a real crypt—with, like, dead people and stuff in it? And you didn't tell us?"

Nick leaned against the wall and slid down until he was sitting on the floor, knees against his chest. "Sorry, I meant to bring it up this morning. Then I forgot with all the Halloween stuff. And after the pool, all anyone could talk about was how I held my breath."

"Sounds like your Halloween wasn't quite as boring as you expected." Angelo nodded thoughtfully. "Is that

where you got the amulet?"

"Yeah." Nick lifted the chain from under his shirt. The red gem was warm against his fingers. "It all started with this cat." For the next twenty minutes he told his friends everything that happened on his trip. Starting with his great-aunt's creepy house, and ending with his strange loss of appetite.

"So, you haven't eaten *anything* since dinner two days ago?" Angelo asked.

"Not much," Nick admitted. "A little turkey meat and a piece of bacon." When he put it that way, it sounded pretty bad. "You think I got a virus in there or something?"

"I'm not sure." Angelo turned to his bookshelf and began pulling down volumes.

Carter scooted a few feet away from Nick. "Man, a virus that kills your appetite. I'd go crazy if I caught that." He gave a hungry glance toward the Halloween bag at the foot of Angelo's bed. "Mind if I have a few of your candy bars? My stuff's all gone."

"You ate your entire bag of candy in one night?" Nick asked. That was excessive even for Carter.

"Most of it." Carter scratched the back of his head. "My parents took away the rest after I threw up."

"Help yourself," Angelo said, without looking away from the book he was poring over.

Carter tore open a Butterfinger, ate half of it in one bite, and waved the rest under Nick's nose. "This isn't tempting at all?"

Nick shook his head. He *was* hungry. And he knew the candy should sound good. His brain remembered liking it. But just the smell made him start to gag.

"Sad, my friend, very, very sad." Carter finished the Butterfinger and ripped open a Hershey's with almonds.

Nick took off the light windbreaker he'd been wearing and set it on the floor. "Does it feel warm in here to you?"

"Nope," Carter said, breaking off squares of chocolate one at a time and tossing them into his mouth. "Maybe you're running a fever. Maybe you've got one of those rare tropical illnesses that eat your flesh."

"I think I might have noticed if something was eating my flesh." Nick scowled. "Besides, how would that explain holding my breath for so long?"

"The rare Cemeteria Dysenteria begins with a loss of appetite," Carter said in a deep announcer's voice. "Then comes increased lung capacity. The virus eats away the patient's entire body, starting with the nose, progressing to the ears, and finally a horrible case of diarrhea that leaves you sitting on the toilet for—"

"Enough." Nick stretched out to kick Carter with the

toe of his shoe. "You're not helping."

"Interesting," Angelo said, holding an old book in his hands.

Carter and Nick looked up. "Did you find something?" Nick asked.

"Maybe." Angelo set the book on his desk, open to a page about three-fourths of the way through, and took something out of his top drawer. "Put this in your mouth," he said, removing a digital thermometer from its plastic case.

Nick took the thermometer and eyed it dubiously. "Is this clean?"

"Disinfected with rubbing alcohol," Angelo said, sounding offended that Nick would even ask. "Push the button and put it under your tongue until it beeps."

While they were waiting, Carter managed to down two more candy bars while recounting the plot of a monster movie he'd watched the day before.

"Rube ettah, ache aray ror annie, rerore re eeb adall," Nick said around his thermometer.

"What did he say?" Carter asked.

The thermometer beeped and Nick took it out of his mouth. "I told Angelo he better take away his candy before you eat it all."

He handed the thermometer to Angelo, who

studied it for a moment before referring to the book again. "Eighty-eight point nine degrees."

"Is that bad?" Nick asked.

"Nearly ten degrees below normal," Angelo said. "If my guess is right, it's going to keep dropping."

Nick started to feel afraid. "*Do* I have some kind of rare virus?"

"Here." Angelo handed an empty water glass to Carter. "Stick the open end against Nick's chest and press your ear to the bottom."

Carter swallowed. "He's not contagious, is he? I mean, no offense, but I think I'd rather die than stop eating."

"Not if it's what I think it is," Angelo said. "But just to be on the safe side, Nick, why don't you put that amulet back inside your shirt."

Nick dropped the chain down his collar while Carter pressed the glass against his chest and listened.

"What am I supposed to be hearing?" Carter asked.

Angelo looked from the book to his watch. A small bead of sweat dripped down his forehead. "Keep listening."

Carter squinched his eyes shut, his forehead wrinkling. For over a minute, no one said a thing. Then Carter's eyes popped open. "I heard something. Not very loud. Kind of a soft *lub-lub*."

"Just what I thought." Angelo took back the glass and set it on the desk. He lifted the book and turned it around so the other boys could see it. "Does this look familiar?"

Nick slid forward across the carpet and studied the picture in the center of the left page. "It's my amulet. My gris-gris."

"It *is* your amulet," Angelo agreed, laying the book down. "But it's not a gris-gris. According to the author, the necklace you're wearing is over a thousand years old. It was created for an African bokor."

"Like a stock broker?" Carter asked.

"Bokor," Angelo corrected. "A bokor is a voodoo sorcerer capable of bringing the dead back to life. Anyone who wears the bokor's amulet becomes cursed."

Nick's hand went to the lump under his shirt. He remembered reading something about a bokor in his aunt's book. "What kind of curse?"

Angelo swallowed. "If my book is right—and from all of your symptoms, I'm pretty sure it is—the moment you put on that amulet you invoked its ancient curse." The house was deathly still. "You are . . . a zombie."

For a second none of the boys said a word. Then they all shouted the same thing at exactly the same time.

"Awesome!"

Nick turned his hands over, looking at the fronts and backs. Other than being a little more pale than normal, they didn't look especially unusual. No flayed skin or protruding bones. "Are you sure?" he asked. "I don't feel like a zombie." But what did a zombie feel like? In the movies they mostly shambled around a lot and grunted. Not a lot to go on there.

"Pretty sure," Angelo said. "It all adds up."

Carter stared at Nick liked he'd never seen him before. "So, you're dead?"

"Technically, *undead*." Angelo pushed his glasses up on his nose. "That's what separates a zombie from your average corpse. His body is slightly higher than room temperature, although it should decrease over time. His heart rate appears to be less than a single beat per minute—causing his cold skin and pale complexion."

That explained a lot, Nick thought. Why his cold shower didn't feel cold, why normal food didn't seem appetizing, and why he didn't need much sleep.

"Have you noticed yourself being more clumsy than usual?" Angelo asked. "Typically a zombie's muscles begin to break down rather quickly."

Nick tried to think. "I might be stumbling a little more than usual. And my hands and feet feel kind of tingly. Like when you lie on your arm and it falls asleep."

"That could be a combination of muscle weakness and poor circulation." Angelo grabbed another book from his shelf. "If I remember right, a zombie's heart beats just enough to keep its blood flowing. Since your flesh isn't really alive, it doesn't need much oxygen."

"That's why you could hold your breath so long!" Carter beamed, a smudge of chocolate marking his chin. "This is *so* cool. We need to call the TV stations and the newspapers. I'll bet they'd pay big bucks for a picture of a real zombie."

"No media," Nick said, getting to his feet.

"Why not?" Carter's smile disappeared. "They'd probably do a special on you."

Nick held up a finger. "Haven't you been paying attention to all the monster movies we've watched? What's the first thing people do when they discover there's a monster in their town?"

Carter slapped his hand to his forehead. "Destroy it."

"Or capture it to do tests," Angelo said.

"I don't want to be anyone's science experiment." Nick shuddered. "And I definitely don't want to have a mob show up at my house with torches and pitchforks."

Angelo nodded. "More like assault rifles, these days."

"Sorry, bad idea," Carter said. He began rooting around in Angelo's Halloween bag looking for something to eat.

Nick's stomach growled. "So what do we do now?"

Angelo began flipping through the pages of his book. "There are plenty of theories in most of these books, but not much hard data. We could learn quite a bit. For example, can zombies communicate with the truly dead? It might be interesting to take you to a cemetery. And how do animals react to you? My dog's in the backyard. The effect of slowed circulation on the rest of the organs might teach us . . ."

As Angelo continued to talk, Nick thought that he'd never realized just how intelligent his friend was. All

those books he read. All those ideas. He studied more than anyone Nick knew and usually got the best scores in the sixth grade. When he was nine, he beat the entire school in a spelling bee. Nick's stomach growled again. "You're really smart," he said.

"What?" Angelo looked up from his book.

Nick licked his lips. "I'll bet your brain is *huge*."

"What's wrong with you?" Carter asked, taking his hand out of the bag.

Nick blinked. "What do you mean?" Why were his friends staring at him so strangely?

"You're . . . *drooling*," Carter said.

"No, I'm not." Nick touched his fingers to his chin and they came away wet. His stomach growled louder than ever.

"Of course." Angelo ran his finger down the page he'd been reading. "You haven't eaten almost anything for nearly two days. You must be starving."

"No, he isn't." Carter laughed. "I just offered him a candy bar."

"Zombies don't eat candy," Angelo said. "They eat flesh and . . . human brains."

Carter's eyes bulged. He clapped his palms over his ears—his bright red hair sticking out from between his fingers—and backed toward the door. "Stay away from

me, you brain-sucking freak. I don't have much to begin with. If you've got to eat someone's brains, start with Angelo's. He's got extra."

"Cut it out," Nick said. "I'm not going to rip open anyone's skull."

"But you *are* going to have to eat," Angelo said. "Even zombies need food."

Nick's stomach growled for the fourth time in the last few minutes. He *was* hungry. And now that he'd identified what it was his stomach wanted, he couldn't stop thinking about brains.

Angelo tapped a fingernail against his teeth in thought. "I guess we could try and find a fresh grave. I don't think they remove a dead person's brain when they embalm him."

"Gross," Nick said. He might be a zombie, but the idea of prying open a coffin for a quick snack was beyond disgusting.

"Maybe we could find some food in your kitchen," Carter suggested, still keeping his distance. "There's got to be something other than human brains a zombie will eat."

"It's possible," Angelo said, clearly uncomfortable there was anything he didn't know for a fact. "The books mostly talk about brains. Still, it might be worth a try."

As the three boys headed down the hall, Nick glanced around. "What's your mom going to think of us poking around her kitchen?"

"She's out in the greenhouse working on cross-pollination of cucumbers," Angelo said. "She wouldn't notice if we blew up the house with dynamite."

Carter opened the Ruizes' refrigerator and poked his head inside. "Yum, coconut cream pie," he said, his voice slightly muted by the door.

"We're looking for food for Nick, not you." Angelo pushed him aside. "Hmm, what about this?" He pulled out a package of hamburger and set it on the counter.

Nick sniffed the meat. It didn't smell as bad as the pancakes had.

Carter rubbed his stomach. "We could fry you up a couple of burgers with onions and pickles and maybe—"

Nick peeled the plastic back and popped a piece of the raw meat into his mouth.

"Disgusting," Carter said, his lips pulling down in a horrified grimace. "That's not even cooked."

Nick's throat tightened as he chewed the raw meat. "It needs to be . . . thicker."

"Let me see." Angelo moved around a few things in the fridge and came out with a plastic bowl. "Leftover

mashed potatoes from Sunday dinner." He dumped the hamburger on top of the potatoes and mixed them around with a big metal spoon.

It was definitely thicker. But now it looked . . . "Too pale."

Carter grabbed a bottle of ketchup and squirted it into the bowl. It was better. Nick stuck in his finger and tried a taste. "Too bland."

Angelo shook in most of a bottle of hot sauce and mixed it all together. Nick stuck a handful of the concoction in his mouth and chewed slowly while Angelo and Carter looked on. "Close," he said. "But there's still something missing."

He walked around the kitchen, sniffing. His sense of smell wasn't strong. But he sensed . . . he wasn't quite sure. He passed the open refrigerator, stuck his head in the pantry, started to turn around, and paused. Something. Something close. He sniffed again and looked down.

There. On the floor. He reached down and snatched up a plastic bowl.

"Dog food," Angelo said in horror. "You want canned dog food?"

Nick scooped the cold, gooey substance into the hamburger and mashed potatoes and mixed it all

together. His stomach rumbled so loudly now it sounded like a wild creature inside of him.

"I think I'm gonna hurl," Carter said, plugging his nose.

Nick grabbed a scoop of the glop with his bare hands and crammed it into his mouth. Then another. And another.

"Yum," he growled, hamburger, potatoes, and dog food spilling from the corners of his lips as he gobbled them down.

It was perfect!

"I've got a *great* idea!" Carter said as the three boys headed to school the next morning.

"Well, there's a first time for everything," Angelo said without looking up from the book he was studying.

"Everybody's a comedian these days." Carter noticed the slice of banana bread Nick's mom had forced into his hand as he walked out the door. "You gonna eat that?"

"No way." Nick handed the slice to Carter and watched in amazement as he wolfed it down in one bite.

"Okay, listen," Carter said around his mouthful of food. "Frankenstein's still mad at us about Halloween. And after what happened yesterday at the pool, he probably thinks we were playing some kind of joke on him, right?"

"I guess so," Nick agreed, although he hadn't really considered it before. Yesterday at the pool had been anything but funny to him.

"So we've got seven more months of watching our backs any time a teacher isn't looking."

Angelo frowned. "Thanks for reminding us."

Carter looked from one friend to the other, practically shaking with excitement. "What if I told you I have a way to stop him from picking on us permanently? Or at least for a couple of months?"

Across the street, Nick noticed a black cat. It wasn't anything special, but instead of chasing leaves or trying to catch birds, it sat perfectly still on the far sidewalk—its eyes tracking the three boys as they walked past. It reminded him a little of—

Carter yanked his jacket sleeve. "Are you listening to me?"

"Yeah," Nick said. "It's just that cat . . ." He looked across the street, where the cat had been, but it was gone.

"I don't see a cat," Angelo said.

Nick looked up and down the sidewalk, but the cat was nowhere to be seen—as if it had never been there.

"Who cares?" Carter yanked his spiky red hair with both hands so it poked up even more than normal. "I'm talking about keeping us from getting beat up and you're looking for a *cat*?"

"Sorry," Nick said. "Tell us your idea." It *was* only a cat, but something about the way it had been watching them made Nick feel like Frankenstein wasn't the only reason they needed to watch their backs.

It turned out Carter's idea actually *was* pretty brilliant. *If* they could pull it off. He was also right about Frankenstein. When Nick walked to the basketball courts at the beginning of first recess, the bully was waiting for him.

"You made me look like an idiot at the pool," Frankenstein said, grabbing Nick by the arm and pulling him close.

At this point Nick normally would have been looking for a yard lady or trying to pull away. But Carter was on the other side of the basketball courts nodding his head and waving his hands. Nick swallowed. "Making you look like an idiot really isn't all that hard."

"What?" Cody's hands tightened as his face turned red. No one ever talked back to him.

Nick's heart would have been pounding if he hadn't been a zombie. As it was, his legs were shaking, though he tried not to show it. "I'm just saying, if you're going to act like an idiot you're probably going to look like one."

"You are so dead, Braithwaite." Frankenstein's jaw went tight and he pulled back his massive fist.

Carter had told Nick to wait at this point, maybe even to let Cody hit him once. But Nick had no intention of finding out whether being undead made punches hurt any less—at least not until he had to. "Today after school," he stammered. "You and me in the woods behind the fence."

Frankenstein's fist hesitated. "You want to . . . *fight* me?"

"You and me, one on one. If you bring your jerk friends though, the fight's off."

The bigger boy blinked as he processed this information. He'd beaten up lots of kids, but Nick wasn't sure anyone had ever actually challenged him to a fight. The bully looked to where Angelo and Carter were watching them. "You gonna bring your friends?"

Nick licked his lips, which had started to peel a little in the last two days. "Just the two of us."

Frankenstein laughed and pushed Nick away. "I

don't think you have the guts to face me alone. I hope your friends do come. Then I can beat you all up at the same time." He sneered. "You chicken out and don't show up, and I promise I'll make it ten times worse."

"I'll be there," Nick said. He really hoped Carter's plan would work.

Carter was thrilled when he heard the fight was on. Even Angelo seemed excited—taking lots of notes in his binder, and saying things like, "I wonder if zombies feel pain once their nerve endings begin to wither?"

Nick, who was going to be doing the dirty work in more ways than one, wasn't nearly as eager. As the clock ticked toward three, his stomach was in knots. He thought most of it was nerves, but some of it must have been hunger, too, because he found himself staring at a boy with an especially large head wondering what his brains might taste like.

As soon as the final bell rang, Nick grabbed his books and raced for the door.

"Good luck," Carter mouthed as Nick hurried by. Angelo gave him a thumbs-up. Easy for them—they weren't the ones who were going to be the punching bag for a hormonally supercharged monster if this scheme didn't work.

The "woods," as most of the kids at school called

them, really weren't much more than a couple dozen scattered oak and eucalyptus trees. The city kept talking about putting in some picnic tables and turning it into a park. For now, it was just a dusty grove behind the school where almost no one came. The perfect place to go of you didn't want anyone to see what you were doing. And a pretty good place for a bully to hide in ambush.

As soon he reached the trees, Nick skidded to a stop and searched for Frankenstein. If Frankenstein had arrived first, the plan would be over before it ever started. Fortunately, he seemed to be alone. That wouldn't last long though; he could already hear the voices of kids shouting and screwing around as they crossed the playground. Cody would be here any minute.

At the far end of the grove was an open ditch where a metal drainage pipe emptied when it rained hard. Nick dropped his backpack at the edge of the ditch. In his pocket was a tube of fake blood Carter had provided. It was the good stuff. The kind they used in movies and upper-end haunted houses.

Nick opened the tube and squeezed a generous amount into his hair—letting it trickle over his forehead and down his face. He quickly scanned the

trees, terrified Frankenstein would appear any second. Squatting in the ditch, he emptied the rest of the tube onto the edge of the metal drainage pipe. Dark red trails dripped down the warm metal and splashed into the dirt.

Squeezing out the last of the blood, he felt like someone was watching him. He scanned the trees but no one was there. Then he saw it. The black cat he'd seen earlier that day was sitting at the end of the ditch. A branch cracked and Nick jerked his head around. Someone was coming! Shoving the tube into his pocket, he dropped to the ground. He positioned himself beneath the open pipe so it looked like he had fallen against it and hit his head. A few seconds later, a voice carried through the trees.

"Hey, wuss-s-s-s-s, where are you?"

The sound of Frankenstein's voice sent chills of terror through Nick's body. Zombie or not, he did not want to see what Cody would do to a kid who actually dared to challenge him.

"Where are you, you little chicken? Did you run home to your mommy already?" The sound of footsteps came closer, and Nick pressed his eyes shut—willing his body to stay perfectly still when what he really wanted was to jump out of the ditch and run for his life.

The footsteps came so close it sounded like Frankenstein was right on top of him. They were accompanied by a meaty *thunking* sound that could only be a palm slamming into a fist. Why had he thought this was a good idea?

"Where are you, you little maggot?" The voice came from right above Nick. He cracked open one eye. Cody was standing at the edge of the ditch, so close Nick could have spit on him—if he wanted to spend the rest of his life in a body cast. All Cody had to do was turn around and he would see Nick lying at the bottom of the ditch. Nick hoped Angelo and Carter were waiting to do their part.

"I knew he'd wuss out." Still facing the other direction, Frankenstein kicked a rock. He started to walk away and Nick wondered if he'd have to groan to get his attention. Then the bully's head tilted. He leaned down and picked something up. "What's this?"

At that moment, Carter and Angelo stepped into the woods. Nick couldn't see them, but he could hear their voices. "Where's Nick?" Angelo said.

Frankenstein stepped away from the edge of the ditch so Nick couldn't see him, either. "That's what I want to know. Your girlfriend said he was going to fight me. He must have chickened out."

"Then what are you doing with his backpack?" Carter demanded.

Lying in the ditch with his arms and legs spread crookedly and his eyes pressed closed, Nick couldn't help but grin a little at how believable his friends sounded. This might actually work.

"I found it on the ground, over by the ditch," Frankenstein said. For the first time since he'd arrived, his voice sounded unsure.

"*Found* it?" Angelo's voice said. "Are you sure you didn't *steal* it, after you beat him up?"

"I didn't touch him," Cody said. "I told you. I found his backpack sitting right there next to the—" The bully's voice cut off suddenly, and Nick could just imagine him looking into the ditch.

The sound of running footsteps came quickly toward the ditch and stopped. For a moment no one said anything.

"Nick!" Carter yelled. Nick could hear rocks and dirt bounce down the side of the ditch as someone climbed down. Nick lay perfectly still, trying his hardest not to smile. Although he didn't need to breathe, his lungs were used to inhaling and exhaling and he had to concentrate to keep his chest from moving.

Hands pressed against his chest and touched his

neck. “He’s not breathing,” Angelo said. “And he doesn’t have a pulse.”

More rocks and dirt tumbled down as someone else climbed into the ditch. Strong hands closed on Nick’s shoulders and he let his head wobble loosely as the bigger boy shook him. “Open your eyes.”

“What did you do to him?” Carter shouted.

“I didn’t do nothing,” Frankenstein said. “He’s faking.” Nick could feel the bully’s breath on his face as he shook him again. It smelled like tuna fish.

“Get back,” Angelo said. Cody released his shoulders and Angelo pried open one of Nick’s eyes. It was all Nick could do not to laugh at his look of fake horror. “His pupils are fixed.”

“Bull,” Frankenstein said, but he sounded shaken.

“Touch his skin,” Angelo said. He grabbed one of Frankenstein’s hands and pressed it against the side of Nick’s face. “It’s cold.”

The bully’s eyes went wide. Nick bit the inside of his cheek. How dumb did you have to be to believe someone’s skin could go cold after being dead for just a few minutes? But clearly Frankenstein did believe. He jerked his palm away.

Angelo gave Nick a wink before sliding his eyelid closed. “Does anyone know CPR?” he shouted.

Nick knew that both Carter and Angelo knew CPR. They learned it at the pool the summer before. But Frankenstein didn't know that.

"You murdered him!" Carter screamed.

"I never touched him." Frankenstein was definitely starting to panic. "I swear."

"Who's going to believe that?" Angelo said. "You came here to beat him up—like you do to everyone. We found you holding his backpack. We've got to go to the police."

"The police?" Frankenstein sounded like he was about to bawl. It served him right. How many kids had he made cry over the years?

For a moment no one spoke. Then Carter said quietly, "They might blame us, too. We knew he was going to fight."

"What should we do?" Frankenstein asked. This was priceless. Nick wished he could be watching it, but he didn't dare open his eyes.

"Carter's right," Angelo said. "We all knew about the fight. We were all here. Cody would be charged with murder. But we could be charged with conspiracy." He was silent, and Nick could imagine Frankenstein hanging on his every word. Angelo was sort of a geek when it came right down to it. But he was so smart everyone

listened to what he said. "We have no choice. We have to bury the body."

Someone let out a sob and Nick wasn't sure whether it was Frankenstein or Carter faking it. "I can't bury a body," a shaking voice said. Definitely Frankenstein.

"You *have* to," Carter said. "Either that, or we go to the police."

The only thing Nick could hear was the sound of heavy breathing. Man, he wished he could see what was going on.

"F-f-fine," Cody stammered. "I'll do it." A second later Nick felt a handful of dirt hit him in the face. Some of it went up his nose and it was all he could do to keep from sneezing.

"Faster!" Carter yelled. "We have to finish the job before someone sees us. Use that board to push dirt on him."

More dirt landed on him. Then more. A rock poked him in the back and he wished he could move around to get a little more comfortable. Soon his entire face was covered. He couldn't be sure, but he thought his arms were covered as well. He hoped his friends hadn't forgotten the second part of the plan. It would totally suck to get buried alive.

"Wait!" Angelo yelled. Under the cover of the dirt,

Nick smiled, then wished he hadn't as bits of soil slipped into his mouth.

"What?" Frankenstein's voice was strangely muffled, and it took Nick a minute to realize why. His ears were full of dirt too.

"I thought I saw him move," Angelo said.

Nick heard someone squeak and was pretty sure it was Frankenstein.

"He couldn't have," the bully said. "You said he was dead."

"He was," Angelo said, his voice serious. "But what if the weight of the dirt started his heart up again?" It was the dumbest thing Nick had ever heard. He was positive even someone as dumb as Frankenstein wouldn't fall for it.

"Someone has to go down and check," Carter said.

"I . . . I can't." Frankenstein sounded about six, and Nick let out a little laugh before he could force his lips shut. Fortunately no one seemed to have heard.

"You have to make sure he's dead and finish the job," Angelo said. "Unless you're too . . . scared."

"Fine." Nick thought he could hear someone climbing into the ditch. He felt a sudden weight on his chest. "What do I do?" Frankenstein asked, his voice trembling.

"Uncover his face and check to see if he's breathing," Angelo called down.

The weight shifted and Nick felt dirt moving around him.

"Put your ear close to his mouth and listen," Carter said.

Nick opened his eyes, ignoring the grit that slid into them.

"I don't hear any—"

Nick waited until Frankenstein turned. Frankenstein saw Nick looking at him. His mouth dropped open. His face lost all color.

"Rrr-aaa-aaaa-argh," Nick growled, doing his best impression of *Night of the Living Dead.*

He had no idea someone that big could move so fast. And he had never heard anyone scream that loud or that high. Before Nick could even sit up, the bully was into the woods—his screams echoing behind him.

"Sounds like the time my mom found a spider in the toilet," Carter said as he and Angelo slid into the ditch and helped Nick out of the hole.

"Did you get pictures?' Nick asked, coughing and trying to comb dirt out of his hair with his fingers.

"Oh, yeah." Angelo held out his digital camera and peered at the screen. "Screaming like a little girl. And

I'm pretty sure that's not apple juice on the front of his pants. He won't be bothering us anymore unless he wants these pictures hanging on every wall of the school."

Carter grinned and slapped Nick on the shoulder. "Mission accomplished."

CHAPTER 15

NEVER UNDERESTIMATE THE POWER OF GIRLS ON A MISSION

Over the next few days Cody Gills was like a ghost of his former tormenting self. Nick and his friends didn't tell anyone what they had done, but every time they came near, the bully scurried in the other direction—his eyes two dark hockey pucks of fear.

When the last bell rang on Friday, Frankenstein was the first one out of the classroom.

"I actually feel kind of sorry for him," Angelo said as the boys zipped up their backpacks and started walking to Nick's house, where they were spending the night. "He knocked the books out of a third grader's hands yesterday."

"So what?" Carter crunched a mouthful of peanut-butter-and-jelly-bean sandwich—his favorite after-school, before-dinner meal. "He always does that."

"Yeah. But this time he apologized and picked them up. And I could swear I saw him flinch when the little kid scowled at him. It's like he's scared of everything now."

Nick knew what Angelo meant. "After all these years I've gotten used to Frankenstein being the bad guy. Now that he's scared of us, it's almost like *we're* the bullies."

"Who cares?" Carter said. "He's been scaring kids for years. We should be named school heroes. Next week I think I'll make him carry my backpack around for me."

"I don't know. It feels wrong." Nick's stomach gurgled. "Do you have any more of the you-know-what at your house?"

Before Angelo could answer, a voice interrupted them. "All right, you three, spill it."

Nick turned to find Angie, Tiffany, and Dana standing right behind them. "What do *you* want?" he asked, wondering how much of the conversation they'd overheard.

Angie Hollingsworth was the smallest of the three girls—a good two inches shorter than Carter—but the

clear leader of her group. She shook back her red hair and smirked. "Like you guys had nothing to do with Frankenstein turning into Chickenstein."

Nick grimaced. He hated to admit it, but Angie was one of the smartest kids in sixth grade. She and Angelo were usually neck and neck for who got the best test scores. That she knew the boys called Cody Gills "Frankenstein" was bad enough. But how could she have already figured out Nick and his friends had something to do with Cody's change of personality?

"We have no idea what you are talking about," Angelo said stiffly. He was a great friend and super-smart, but a terrible liar.

Angie tilted her head and held out her hand. "Then you won't mind me seeing what's inside that notebook you've been scribbling in so much lately?"

Angelo pulled the monster notebook close to his chest.

Carter tried to talk and swallow at the same time and ended up choking on his sandwich. Nick pounded Carter's back and a slobbery orange jelly bean flew out of his mouth onto the sidewalk.

"That's disgusting," Dana Lyon said, wrinkling her nose. Dana was nearly as tall as Angelo, with sandy blond hair and blue eyes. She was a natural athlete who

starred in track, volleyball, and softball.

"Not as disgusting as your face." Carter wiped orange spit off his chin with the back of his hand.

"It's not like everyone in school doesn't know you guys did something to Cody," Tiffany said. Nick thought she might have been looking at him. But behind her giant pink sunglasses, it was impossible to tell. Tiffany Staheli had long dark hair that was always done in the latest style. She was the second-best dresser in school—only slightly behind Kimber Tidwell, a girl so popular she managed to convince all the other kids to call kindergarten *Kimber*-garden when she was six.

Unfortunately, Tiffany was also in on all the latest school gossip. If *she* said everyone knew Nick and his friends had something to do with Cody's change, it was probably true.

"That's not all," Angie said, folding her arms across her chest. She stared at Nick as though trying to read his thoughts. "There's something different about you, Braithwaite."

Nick realized he hadn't been breathing and quickly sucked air into his lungs, trying to look more normal.

"There's something different about *you*, too," Carter said. "You're so short you look like somebody chopped off your legs at the knees and put ugly shoes on the stumps."

"Look who's talking," Dana said. "If doctors put warning labels on candy, your picture would be on every wrapper. 'Caution: Sugar may stunt your growth and make your hair look like you used spray paint instead of hair spray.'"

"Hilarious." Carter bunched his fists, but Nick was pretty sure Dana could take his friend in a fight.

"If you want to know what the deal is with Cody, go ask him," Nick said.

Tiffany tilted down her sunglasses and looked at Nick over them. "Kimber did. And she says that when she brought up your name he turned white as a Vera Wang wedding gown and wouldn't say another word."

Nick had no idea who or what Vera Wang was, but he got the point. "So what if we *did* have something to do with it? Why do you care? It's not like anyone's going to miss having Franken—I mean Cody—beating on them."

Angie stepped forward until she was so close Nick could smell her strawberry-scented shampoo. "Something about this whole thing stinks. And it's not just that you smell like you haven't bathed in a week. First there was that thing at the pool. Then the biggest bully in school is suddenly scared to death of you. And whatever you say, there's something different about you, ever since you came back from your aunt's funeral."

Nick gulped. He knew Angie was smart, but this was way too close to the truth. How did Angie even know that he'd gone to his aunt's funeral? If she'd figured this much out, he knew it wouldn't be long until she managed to put the rest of the pieces together. Especially since she and her friends were nearly as crazy about monsters as Nick, Carter, and Angelo were.

Trying to look like he couldn't care less whether she believed him or not, he opened his mouth. What he meant to say was "You need to get a life of your own and stop spending so much time sticking your nose into mine." What came out was "Lunchtime shoe wax, fluorescent bra strap. Slippery toe croak peach pit."

"What?" Angie said, taking a step back. "Are you mocking me?"

Nick's eyes went wide and he slapped his hand to his mouth.

What was that? Angelo mouthed silently.

Nick had no idea. It was like his brain had come disconnected from his tongue. Terrified he'd somehow lost his ability to speak, he opened his mouth and tried again.

"I. Have. To. Go," he said, speaking each word carefully. "I. Have. Home. Work. To. Do."

Angie narrowed her eyes and shook her head.

"Don't think I won't figure out whatever you're up to."

"Gotta. Go." Nick turned away and hurried up the street before he could do anything else that might give away his zombieness.

Just as Nick and his friends reached the corner, Angie yelled, "I'm going to be watching you." And then, "See you tomorrow night."

"Dude, what was that all about?" Carter burst out as soon as they were around the corner.

"Shhh." Angelo looked over his shoulder to make sure they were no longer in hearing distance of the girls.

"Fluorescent bra strap?" Carter said, just as loudly. "Seriously? Were you *trying* to make them more suspicious than they already were?"

Nick shook his head. "I don't know what happened. I was just mopping when suddenly the wrong words started coming out."

"You were just *what*?" Carter asked with an odd little smile on his face.

"Talking," Nick said. "Why are you grinning like that?"

"You said *mopping*." Carter giggled.

"I did not." Nick looked to Angelo, who shrugged and nodded.

"Sorry." Angelo rubbed his chin. "You definitely said *mopping*, not *talking*."

Nick touched his throat as though it were some strange instrument he was learning how to play for the first time. "What's wrong with me?"

Angelo flipped open his notebook and began writing. "I can't say for sure until I've done some more research. But my guess is that you are experiencing early signs of synaptic breakdown around your sylvian fissure."

"Sylvia who?" Carter screwed up his face.

"Not a who. A what," Angelo said. "The sylvian fissure is the part of the brain dividing the frontal and parietal lobe. The part of the cortex around the sylvian fissure is thought to be involved in spoken language. In the event of a synaptic breakdown the neurons would be unable to—"

"Stop," Nick said. "You're making my head hurt worse than it already does. Explain in words two syllables or less."

Angelo thought for a moment. "You're having brain farts."

"Oh, that's *much* more helpful," Nick said sarcastically.

Angelo closed his notebook. "It was only a matter of time really. As your body shuts down, your mind goes with it. Eventually zombies' minds and bodies deteriorate to the point that they no longer think at all but merely shamble around following the scent of human flesh."

"Sounds kind of fun," Carter said. Nick raised an eyebrow and Carter added, "Well, maybe not the human flesh part. But the mindless thing would be cool. No more homework. No more studying. No more math lessons. No more having to think at all."

"You're well on the way to that and you're not even a zombie." Angelo grinned, then looked closely at Nick. "Have you noticed any other changes?"

Nick shook his head. "I don't think so."

"What about that thing on your elbow?" Carter tugged at the sleeve of Nick's shirt, revealing a gaping wound.

Nick tried to twist his arm around so he could see the back of it. His shoulder felt oddly loose in its socket and made a kind of groaning sound as he turned it. "I fell a couple of days ago shooting hoops."

"A couple of *days* ago?" Carter plugged his nose.

"Dude, it hasn't even scabbed over and it smells worse than the sweat socks my little brother only changes when my mom peels them off his feet."

Angelo leaned closer to get a better look. "Does this hurt?" he asked, poking the unhealed cut with the back of a pen.

Nick cringed, anticipating a jolt of pain, but the truth was he could hardly feel it. "Not really. In fact, now that you mention it, my arm didn't hurt all that much even when I scraped it."

Angelo nodded as if that was exactly what he'd expected to hear. "Your body's healing systems are slowing down along with your heartbeat and breathing. Nerve endings are dying. Cells are no longer reproducing. Basically, your body is discovering it's no longer alive and it's beginning to decompose."

"Whoa!" Carter gulped down the last of his sandwich and beamed with delight. "That is *so* cool. What if your skin starts peeling off? Maybe you could get a bone to poke out too. Imagine how scared of you Frankenstein would be then."

"Along with every other kid in the school, and the teachers," Angelo said.

"Not to mention my parents." Nick groaned. His mom had already started looking at him funny. It was

only a matter of time before she decided he must be sick and took him to a doctor. He fingered the amulet under his shirt. "It's been pretty cool being a zombie. But maybe it's time I started to think about taking this off."

"I call second!" Carter shouted. "Promise me you'll let me try it next. I totally want to pull off my arm and sew it onto the middle of my back."

As the three boys reached the top of the hill that overlooked Nick's house, a large yellow truck came into view.

"What's with the moving truck?" Carter asked. "You're not going anywhere again, are you?"

"Not that I know of." Nick was positive his parents wouldn't decide to move without telling him, but cold sweat dripped down his back until he realized the men were carrying pieces of furniture out of the truck and into his house. "It's just the furniture my parents had shipped back from my aunt's house," he said with a sigh of relief.

"Looks sort of old and beat up," Carter said.

"I know." Nick nodded. "I don't know what my parents see in any of it."

Angelo peered into the dim back of the truck. "Did you bring back any of your Aunt Lenore's voodoo items?"

"No. My parents made sure all the good stuff got thrown away."

"What a waste."

"Lend a hand or get out of the way," Nick's dad called, coming around from the side of the truck. "This is a working zone. Men are breaking a sweat here."

Nick noticed his dad was carrying a lamp that might have weighed five pounds at the most.

Catching Nick's look, his dad gripped the base of the lamp, which was shaped like a large black-and-red bird, in both hands. "I'm carrying the valuable items while they carry the bulk. Tomorrow, I want you to help me get all this stuff put away. My boss is coming for dinner."

"Sure thing," Nick promised.

"By the way," Dad called over his shoulder, "there's a letter for you inside the front door."

Nick glanced at his friends. Who would send him a letter? As soon as he saw the envelope on the entryway table though, he knew who had sent it. The canary-yellow paper was a dead giveaway.

"Nice desk," Carter said as the three boys passed though Nick's living room, which was packed wall to wall with furniture.

Nick, who was already starting up the stairs, barely heard him. As soon as the three boys got into his

bedroom, Nick closed the door and turned the letter over in his hands. There was no return address and the only writing on the front was Nick's name and address, written in an oddly formal handwriting that looked like the kind of thing you might see on the front of a wedding invitation. But he had no doubt who it was from.

"What's the big deal?" Carter asked. "Love letters from some long-lost girlfriend you never told us about?" He pretended to sniff the air. "Is that the aroma of perfume I smell? Or did you just swipe your mom's deodorant today?"

"It's not a love letter," Nick said. "It's from this guy. . . ." He tried to think of a good way to describe Mazoo. "He was this big dude in a bright yellow suit."

"Sounds like Tiffany's kind of guy," Carter said.

Nick ignored him. "He was my aunt's pastor and he performed her funeral service. But he was also in her house. He asked me if I had explored it. I think he might have been one of those voodoo sorcerer guys. A . . ."

"A bokor?" Angelo had been flipping through an encyclopedia of fantastical creatures on Nick's desk. He dropped the book and hurried over to where Nick had started to tear the letter open and held out a hand. "You might want to be careful where you do that."

Nick paused and looked at the envelope. "You think it's cursed or something?"

Angelo bit his lip. "Does he have any reason to curse you?"

"I don't think so." Nick tried to remember anything Mazoo had said to him. "He told me I was a lot like my aunt. Then he asked if I had looked around her house and wanted to know if I had any questions." There was something else too, but he couldn't remember what.

"Maybe he thought you were a bokor too," Angelo said, his eyes serious. "He could have been testing you. If he thought you were a competitor, this could be his chance to get you out of the way."

Nick swallowed. He shook the envelope. "It doesn't feel like there's anything inside."

"It could be a powder so fine you can't feel it," Angelo said. "Or it might be something in the ink. Or a curse that only affects you when you read it."

The letter seemed to be getting heavier and heavier in Nick's hand. "What should I do?" he asked. "Should I throw it away or burn it?"

The three boys looked at one another. Angelo almost always had an answer for everything. But now he appeared as unsure as his friends.

"I can't stand it," Carter blurted. Before anyone could stop him, he grabbed the bright yellow letter and ripped it open. Wide-eyed, he reached inside and pulled out a piece of stationery the same color as the

envelope. But his hands were shaking so badly he dropped the paper and it seesawed slowly to the floor. For a moment, it seemed that it would land facedown. But just as it was about to hit the ground, a breeze flipped it over.

All three boys held their breath. The handwriting on the page was the same as that on the envelope. There was only a single line.

The owl has the answers you seek.

Carter reached up to touch his face. "Am I cursed?" he asked softly. "Is my face . . . hideous?"

Nick looked at Angelo and they both burst into nervous laughter.

"*I* wouldn't want to look like that," Angelo said. "But I think *you're* stuck with it."

Carter's ears went bright red. "Very funny."

Nick picked up the letter.

"What does it mean?" Angelo asked.

"No idea." Nick turned the paper over. Maybe there was invisible ink on the back? "I think he said something like that at the funeral, too. Something about the owls having wisdom. But what owls?"

"Owls represent birth and death in many cultures,"

Angelo said. "They are also viewed as familiars in witchcraft."

Nick couldn't imagine any way that might apply to him.

"The innuits viewed owls as sources of guidance," Angelo added.

Nick scratched his head. "I'm not an innuit."

"Or maybe he's talking about the owls on the desk," Carter said.

Nick and Angelo stared at him.

"The one downstairs."

Carter led Nick and Angelo down to the Braithwaites' living room. It looked like an antique shop, filled from one end to the other with old furniture. The movers, who had carried in the last few pieces while the boys were in Nick's room, were standing in the front yard discussing something with Nick's parents.

"See, right here," Carter said, weaving through the odds and ends until he reached a roll top desk with an owl on each corner. It was the desk from Aunt Lenore's basement. But what was it doing here? Mom had been determined that everything from the basement should be destroyed.

Nick hurried to the desk and began pulling open drawers. There was nothing in any of them. "Someone

must have emptied it," he said, disappointment burning in his stomach.

"But the owls are cool," Carter said. "They look like they're watching you." He reached to one of the glaring heads. At his touch, the head turned. There was an audible click as a section of the desk slid open, and a small gold bottle dropped onto the floor.

Carter picked up the thumb-sized bottle and bounced it in his palm as though he'd known it was there all along. "So is this what you were looking for?"

For the rest of the night, the boys worked at discovering what the tiny gold bottle was and how to use it. The top was sealed over and they couldn't figure out any way to open it. They twisted and turned it. They shook it, squeezed it, and tapped the sides. They examined it under a magnifying glass, a microscope, and even a black light. The last was Carter's idea, and none of them had any clue what it was supposed to reveal. But they tried it anyway.

It seemed to be hollow, and if you were very quiet and shook it, you could hear a faint rattling coming from inside. But other than that, they were stumped.

Sometime after two in the morning, Carter and

Angelo finally fell asleep. When they woke up a little after ten Saturday morning, Nick was spinning the bottle like a top on the surface of his desk.

Angelo rubbed his eyes. "Any luck?"

"Nada," Nick muttered, letting the object clink to a stop against the base of his lamp.

Carter yawned and ran his fingers through his spiky hair. "Didn't you sleep at all?" he croaked.

"Don't need to," Nick said. "Even when I try, all I do is lie awake on my pillow."

"Maybe we could use acid on it," Angelo said. "I've got some at home in my chemistry set."

"Or we could hit it with a sledgehammer and bash it open." Carter pretended to swing a heavy hammer over his shoulder.

Nick cupped the bottle protectively in his hand. "I don't think Mazoo hid it there for me to smash or dissolve. There has to be something we're missing."

Angelo picked up the object and turned it between his fingers. "What makes you think Mazoo hid it?"

"Who else could have done it? He's the one who sent me the letter."

"He told you where to find it," Angelo said in a low, mysterious voice, like a detective in an old movie. "But you don't know he hid it in the desk."

Nick pressed his hands to his eyes. Although he wasn't tired, his head throbbed from thinking too hard and a dull ache in his stomach reminded him he hadn't eaten anything in more than a day. "If Mazoo didn't put it there, who did?"

Angelo set the bottle back on the desk and twisted the ends of an imaginary mustache. "To solve the mystery of the bottle, you must think like the bottle."

Carter shook his head sadly. "All that reading has finally affected his brain. I say we go to the gas station and buy a bunch of those ninety-nine-cent burritos."

"Inspector Ruiz needs no food. He lives for the chase. Think about it. You found the bottle in the desk. Whoever put it there must have known about the hiding place. Clearly Mazoo knew about it, but he could have given it to you at the funeral instead of going to all the trouble of hiding it. Therefore it stands to reason that the bottle belongs to someone who knew about the hiding place but couldn't give you the bottle in person, because . . . she was dead."

Nick hated it when Angelo went all brainiac on them, but this time he had a point. "You think it belongs to Aunt Lenore?"

Angelo beamed and touched his finger to the tip of his nose.

"Maybe it's a secret message," Carter said, now wide-awake. "Maybe she's trying to tell you who her murderer is."

Nick snorted. "She wasn't murdered. She died of a heart attack."

"Do you know that for *sure*?" Carter asked.

Nick opened his mouth before realizing he didn't. His parents told him his aunt had died of a heart attack. But how did they know? Did Mazoo tell them? Maybe she'd been killed by her own snake venom. Maybe that's why it was in the basement. And even if she didn't, even if she was checked out by a real doctor, would he be able to tell the difference between a normal heart attack and one brought on by some kind of voodoo curse? "But why would someone want to kill her?"

"You tell us," Angelo said. "You're the one who knew her."

"Not really. I didn't even know I had a great-aunt until my parents told me." Nick bit at the edge of his thumbnail as a thought occurred to him. "There was a book though—almost completely burned up in her fireplace. I thought it was weird she would have left it there."

Angelo and Carter leaned close. "What kind of book?"

"A journal, I think." Nick wished he'd had more time to look at it before his parents walked in on him. "There was something about a bokor who was trying to come back from the grave. I think she called him the King. And someone named E who had given in to something."

"Dude, you're giving me goose bumps." Carter ran his hand over the back of his arm where all the tiny hairs stood on end.

"Why didn't you tell us this before?" Angelo asked, opening his notebook.

"I meant to, but then I found the amulet and the whole zombie thing happened and I forgot all about it. There was something else, too. Something about a key and a treasure."

Carter's mouth dropped open. "Like a *buried* treasure?"

"I don't know," Nick admitted. "My parents walked in before I could finish reading and now I'll probably never find out."

Angelo tapped the tip of his pen slowly against his monster notebook. "Maybe your aunt killed some kind of voodoo king for his treasure. And maybe he could come back from the grave because he's a zombie like you. That amulet you're wearing could be part of his treasure. It could be he killed your aunt to get it back."

"If he did," Carter said, "he's probably after you now that you have the amulet."

Nick tried to think it all through. But his brain seemed to be running at half speed lately. "How does Mazoo fit in? If he's a bad guy, he could have grabbed me any time he wanted at the funeral."

"Except you didn't have the amulet yet," Angelo said.

That was true. If Mazoo was trying to get the amulet, he would have had to wait until after Nick discovered it in the graveyard. "Why would Mazoo tell me about the desk though?"

"No clue." Angelo picked up the gleaming metal bottle. "But your Aunt Lenore was a voodoo queen, right?"

Nick and Carter nodded.

"So let's say she wanted to get you a message. Wouldn't she use voodoo to do it?"

"You think the bottle is some kind of charm or something?" Nick asked. It did make a strange kind of sense.

"I don't know," Angelo said. "But I do know someone who might."

• • •

"I'm sorry," the woman behind the reference desk said. "But Mr. Blackham won't be in until four."

Nick looked at the clock on the library wall. It wasn't even two yet.

"That's okay," Angelo said. "We'll come back then." The three boys found a table far enough away from any other readers that no one could overhear them.

"You want to ask a *librarian* about voodoo?" Carter asked, the skepticism clear in his voice.

"Not just *any* librarian," Angelo said. "Mr. Blackham is a professional historian. People all around the world hire him to research crazy stuff."

"Why not just look it up yourself in a toilet?" Nick said.

Angelo's forehead wrinkled and Carter snickered.

"I mean a book," Nick said. It was annoying to think one thing and have your mouth say something completely different. "There are lots of books around here. Why do we have to wait?"

"We can look," Angelo said. "But some of the best books—the really old ones—are kept in the back and they don't let just anyone see them."

Nick guessed he didn't mind. It wasn't like he had anything else to do. And besides, at least they had stopped to get something to eat before coming here.

He'd finished off the last of the brain substitute—licking the final bits of red hamburger and dog food off the inside of the container—so his stomach wasn't growling like a broken vacuum cleaner anymore.

For the next two hours, the boys pored over all the books they could find on voodoo, treasures, or zombies. It turned out Angelo had checked them all out before and he was right. None of them had anything that might provide any information about the gold bottle.

At exactly four o'clock, a shadow dropped over the table. Nick looked up to see a pale man with slick black hair and piercing black eyes. He was wearing a strange-looking coat that had normal sleeves but came down to his knees, like a superhero's cape. Not that Nick had ever seen a superhero dressed all in black—unless you considered Zorro a superhero. And this guy definitely wasn't Zorro.

"I understand you are looking for me." The man's voice was somehow both soft and penetrating at the same time.

Nick wasn't sure he could talk. Something about the man's eyes freaked him out a little.

Fortunately Angelo spoke up. "Mr. Blackham. These are my friends, Nick and Carter. We need your

advice on something. Nick's great-aunt died last week. When Nick went to the funeral in Louisiana, he discovered a bunch of weird stuff in her basement. We think she might be a—"

Nick shot Angelo a warning look. How did he know they could trust this guy? Or that he'd even believe them if they could?

The tall man nodded as if Nick had spoken the questions out loud, and tapped his chin. "A voodoo queen?"

Carter's mouth dropped open. "How could you possibly know that?"

"I pay attention to what my patrons read," the man said, tilting his chin toward the table where they'd been studying.

Had he been spying on them? Nick's heart leaped into his throat at the thought of this strange man watching them without their knowledge. But he also felt a surge of hope. If the librarian knew about their suspicions and was still willing to talk with them, maybe he was more than he appeared.

"We can trust him," Angelo said. "He knows about all kinds of strange stuff."

They'd only just met the man, but already Nick was beginning to feel the same way. There was something about Mr. Blackham that made Nick sense the

librarian wouldn't laugh at them, no matter how crazy their story might sound. "She left me something." Nick reached into his pocket, but the man quickly put up a hand encased in a black leather glove.

"Not here. Come into my office." Mr. Blackham nodded at the woman behind the reference desk. "See that we are not disturbed." And he led the boys through a maze of shelves and tall stacks of books.

At last they came to a large metal desk tucked into a kind of alcove at the back of the library. The desk was covered with not only books but also statues, arrowheads, maps, bits of broken pottery, and even a large rusty dagger. On the front of the desk, a nameplate read BARTHOLOMEW BLACKHAM, REFERENCE LIBRARIAN.

"Now then," he said, settling himself into a deep leather chair behind the desk, "find a seat and tell me everything."

Find was right. All of the chairs were buried beneath huge mounds of books and papers. It took nearly five minutes for the boys to clear them off.

Once they were seated, Angelo told the librarian everything. Nick waited for the man to laugh or disagree when Angelo told him about Nick turning into a zombie, but the man barely blinked an eye. It was

almost like he knew everything Angelo was going to say before he said it.

When Angelo had finished speaking, Mr. Blackham pulled off his gloves one finger at a time. "Very interesting."

"You believe us?" Nick asked.

"Why wouldn't I?" the man said. Which Nick realized wasn't exactly an answer. "You wouldn't know it to look at this city now, but Pleasant Hill was once known as Oddville."

"Oddville?" Carter sputtered. "What kind of a name is that?"

The man nodded as though Carter had asked exactly the right question. "The kind of name for a place where things aren't always as they appear." He laid his gloves on the desk and tilted his head toward Nick. "May I see the item your aunt left you?"

Nick dug into his pants pocket and pulled out the bottle.

Mr. Blackham turned the metal object over, sniffed it, shook it near his ear, and even touched it with the tip of his tongue.

Nick hadn't thought of tasting it. "Do you know what it is?"

Mr. Blackham nodded, his dark eyes even blacker in

the shadows here at the back of the library. "Have you ever heard of *gros-bon-ange*?" he asked. All three boys shook their heads.

"Translated literally, it means 'great good angel.' Along with the *ti-bon-ange*, 'little good angel,' it is thought by some people to make up the human soul. The *gros-bon-ange* is the body's life force that remains after a person dies."

Nick stared at the bottle as his mouth went dry.

Mr. Blackham set the object on the desk. "This is a *pot tet*, a head jar. Normally it would be made of crockery or porcelain. Inside is probably a lock of hair, a fingernail, perhaps a bit of clothing. The *pot tet* is used to hold the *gros-bon-ange* until it can be released to return to the cosmic energy where it came from."

"That's my aunt's . . ." Nick's throat was so tight he couldn't get out the word.

The librarian smiled. His teeth were very long and very white. "Her soul. Or at least part of it." He handed the gold bottle back to Nick, who felt a little uncomfortable holding it. It was like holding the ashes of someone who'd been cremated.

"Normally the pot would be opened by a loved one and the soul released," Mr. Blackham said. "But whoever created this seems to have gone to great pains to

keep it sealed. If she wanted you to have it, there must be a very important reason." He reached under his desk, pulled out a heavy black book, and handed it to Angelo. "Be careful with this. It's quite irreplaceable."

"Will the book tell me how to open this?" Nick asked.

Mr. Blackham seemed surprised by the question. "Absolutely not. I have no idea how to open your aunt's *pot tet*. Or even if it can be opened. The book says nothing about that."

"Then what good is it?" Nick asked. "And what am I supposed to do with the *pot tet*?"

"Perhaps we can discuss that another time," Mr. Blackham said. "But I'm afraid you're rather late."

"Late for wh—"

Nick's words were cut off by the ringing of a phone on Mr. Blackham's desk. The librarian reached beneath a thick stack of papers and pulled out a phone receiver that looked at least fifty years old. "Yes?" he said, holding the phone to his ear. "He is." He nodded. "I'll send him right away."

Mr. Blackham returned the phone to the stack of papers and smiled at Nick. "It seems you are late for dinner."

"Oh my gosh!" Nick jumped up from the desk. He'd totally forgotten that tonight his dad's boss was coming over for dinner. He'd promised to help clean up. "Gotta go," he called, turning and racing toward the door.

He ran all the way home and arrived at the house trembling and covered with sweat. Apparently even zombies could get tired if they worked hard enough.

Mom was waiting just inside the front door when he walked in. "Do you have any idea what time it is? I've been calling all over trying to find you. Thank goodness at least Angelo tells his mother where he's going."

The living room was no longer filled with furniture,

and Nick remembered he was supposed to have helped move it. "Sorry," he said. "I lost track of boxer shorts. I mean time." His mother's eyes narrowed, but before she could say anything he started toward the stairs. "I'll go clean up."

"Change into a shirt and tie. And hurry. Mr. Ferguson is going to be here in fifteen minutes."

"I have to wear a tie?" he whined. He hated ties. They made him feel like he couldn't breathe—even if he didn't exactly have to breathe.

"Yes, you do," Mom said, sorting through a handful of silverware. She looked in Nick's direction and sniffed. "Take a shower too, and use some of your dad's cologne. Maybe it's a teenage boy thing, but you smell like the chimpanzee cages at the zoo."

Dad walked out of the kitchen carrying a steaming bowl. "That might not be such a bad thing. Mr. Ferguson's bringing his niece. She's about your age and I hear she loves chimps."

Nick's mouth dropped open. *Niece?* No one had said anything about his dad's boss bringing a girl to dinner. One look from his mom though and he knew arguing would be a very bad idea. Instead he stomped into his room, muttering to himself about the unfairness of being expected to have dinner with a girl.

By the time he was showered, changed, and sprinkled with a liberal amount of his dad's cologne—which Nick personally thought smelled even worse than decomposing flesh—it was a few minutes after six. He walked into the dining room to see that his dad's boss had already arrived. Mr. Ferguson and his wife were sitting down at the table as Nick's dad told one of his long-winded jokes. Mrs. Ferguson, who looked about the same age as Nick's mom, was dressed in a fancy black dress and pearls. Mr. Ferguson, who was almost completely bald, wore a dark gray suit. Seated beside them was a girl with red hair who looked strangely familiar, although Nick couldn't see her face from that angle.

Dad finished his joke, and Mr. and Mrs. Ferguson laughed politely.

"John and Danyelle," Mom said, clearly relieved to change the subject, "this is our son, Nicholas."

Nick scowled at the use of his full name. He scowled even more when the girl turned around and he realized why she looked so familiar. It was Angie Hollingsworth.

"I understand you and our niece go to school together," Mrs. Ferguson said.

"Um, yeah," Nick muttered. So that's what she'd meant when she'd told him she'd see him tomorrow

night. How could his parents make him have dinner with *Angie,* of all people? Angie smirked at him as Nick took the only open seat beside her.

Dad grinned like this was the best news ever. "So you two are friends?"

"Oh, yes," Angie said, batting her eyes and pretending to be thrilled. As Nick sat down, she leaned over to him and whispered, "You smell like a dead fish."

"You look like one," he whispered back with a fake smile.

"You two kids must have a lot in common," Mrs. Ferguson said as Dad sliced the roast beef.

"Not really," Nick started to say, but Angie cut him off.

"We do." Angie gave him a look that made it clear she knew he couldn't disagree in front of his dad's boss. "In fact, he was telling us all about his exciting trip to Louisiana. I'd love to hear more about it."

"Is that right?" Mom gave Nick a tight smile that he could read all too well. *Don't bring up any voodoo talk unless you want to be grounded until you're old enough to vote.*

She didn't need to worry. He had no intention of giving Angie any more information than she already had. "Just a bunch of bald-headed monkeys." Nick's

dad gave a strained laugh and Nick realized what he'd just said as his mom's elbow jabbed him in the ribs. "I mean mosquitoes and alligators."

Mr. Ferguson ran a hand over his smooth scalp. "I see."

"I've heard some people still practice voodoo out there," Angie said. "You know, spells and charms and . . . *curses.*"

Nick felt his stomach drop. Did she know something or was she guessing?

Nick's dad looked pale. "Nick didn't say anything about—*ouch*!" Dad glanced at Mom, who Nick was pretty sure had just kicked him under the table, and suddenly focused on passing around food.

Mom tapped her lips gently as she passed Dad the mashed potatoes. "Richard was going to say that his aunt had some lovely pieces of furniture."

"Isn't that nice," Mrs. Ferguson said, spooning dressing over her salad.

Angie spooned some baby carrots onto her plate and handed them to Nick. "What were you three doing at the library today?" she whispered.

"You were *spying* on us?" he whispered back, taking as few vegetables as he could get away with.

As Dad and Mr. Ferguson launched into a conversation about someone who worked in the marketing

department, Nick noticed his mother was watching him and Angie closely. A clear sign that he better not say anything rude if he valued life as he knew it. This was going to be the worst night ever. Not only did he have to make it look like he was actually eating something, but he also had to listen to Angie's trash-talking without saying anything rude back.

"I told you we'd be watching." Angie took a piece of roast beef from the platter. "Tiffany says you guys spent a long time reading up on voodoo. Care to explain why?"

"I don't have to explain anything," Nick said, searching for the rarest piece of meat he could find before passing the platter to his mother. "And I don't know how much I'd trust Tiffany. As far as I can tell, she's never read anything but fashion magazines and makeup instructions."

Nick tried not to show it, but he was worried. He could rip on the girls all he wanted, but the truth was, they were smart. And sooner or later they were going to realize what the boys were up to. They would have already if the idea of Nick being an actual zombie wasn't so completely crazy.

"Potatoes?" Mom said.

Nick took the mashed potatoes from his mother and the big bowl nearly slipped out of his fingers. Something

was wrong. He could barely feel the bowl's smooth surface. It was like his hands were numb. Gripping the spoon was like trying to squeeze an ice cube with a pair of chopsticks. He put as small a pile of potatoes as he could onto his plate and gratefully handed the bowl to Angie.

"Klutz," she whispered.

As Angie reached for the bowl, Nick noticed the tip of something small and pink sticking up out of the pile of fluffy white potatoes. For a second he thought a baby carrot had fallen into the bowl. Then he looked at his right hand—the hand he had spooned the potatoes with. With mounting horror, he realized something was missing. His thumb and first three fingers looked normal. But his smallest finger—his pinky—was gone.

His eyes darted from the stump where his little finger should have been to the small pink tip sticking out of the potatoes. It was his finger. His pinky had fallen into the potatoes that first Angie, then Mrs. Ferguson, then his father's boss were about to dish onto their plates.

Angie looked at him, perplexed. Clearly she knew something was wrong—just not what, yet. But he could imagine her shriek the moment she looked down at the potatoes and spotted the fingernail pointing up at her. Ordinarily that would have been something he'd look

forward to. Not now. As soon as she realized what had happened, Angie would figure the whole thing out. And once *she* knew Nick was a zombie, she'd blab to everyone.

Angie's gaze left his and started toward the mashed potatoes. There was no way he could get his finger back without everyone noticing. Any second, Angie would spot it. How could he explain that? He searched for a solution, but there was only one he could come up with. Angie's hands closed around the bowl. Knowing this was not going to turn out well, Nick did the only thing he could think of.

With all his might, he shoved the bowl up and out. Angie's eyes went wide. Her mouth opened in a small "oh" of shock. Nick watched with horror as the bowl sailed into the air. Potatoes flew everywhere. Some hit Angie in the face. A spray of white dots splattered across Mrs. Ferguson's black dress like machine-gun fire. A mound of potatoes as big as Nick's fist landed with a wet plop on Mr. Ferguson's head.

Before anyone could respond, Nick dived to the floor, scooping up his finger and tucking it safely into his pocket. That's when the yelling started.

"Guys, over here," Nick whispered, waving out his bedroom window to Carter and Angelo, who were wheeling their bikes up the front walk. It was early enough Sunday morning that his parents weren't up yet, but he didn't want to take any chances.

The boys dropped their bikes on the front lawn and walked to the window. "What's with all the secrecy?" Carter asked. "First you call us at five-thirty a.m. and won't tell us why, and now you're whispering out the window like we shouldn't even be here."

Nick glanced over his shoulder. Still keeping his voice low he said, "We've got a problem." He handed something out the window to Angelo.

"Holy crapolla," Carter said, realizing what Angelo was holding. "Is that what I think it is?"

Nick stuck out his right hand with its small pink stump.

Angelo turned the finger over, examining the severed end like it was nothing more than an especially interesting biology project. "It was only a matter of time, I guess. When did it come off?"

Nick rolled his eyes. "Come through the side door. But don't wake up my parents."

Nick told them the whole story as the three boys sat in his room. Carter, sprawled out on the beanbag chair in the corner, shook his head and scrounged through what was left of the Halloween candy his parents had returned to him. "Man, what I wouldn't give to have seen Angie get a face full of mashed potatoes."

"Do you think she saw the finger?" Angelo asked.

Nick shook his head. "Things happened too fast. My dad wasn't exactly thrilled that I dumped dinner on his boss, but no one suspects I did it on purpose. I told them the bowl slipped out of my fingers." He took his pinky from Angelo. "So what are we gonna do? If I take the amulet off, what happens to my finger?"

Carter started searching through Nick's desk. After a bit of digging, he came up with a big silver roll.

"Duct tape?" Nick asked, clutching his pinky protectively to his chest. "You want to put my finger on with duct tape?"

"Why not?" Carter said. "My dad once held half his car's front bumper on with duct tape."

"Yeah, well, call me crazy, but I think there might be a little difference between your dad's bumper and my finger."

Angelo thought for a minute. "Get me some fishing line and a sewing needle."

When Nick came back with the items, Angelo had him put his hand under the stand-mounted magnifying glass they used for attaching small model parts.

"That's awesome!" Carter said. "Why don't you sew it onto his left hand? Then he could be one of those guys with four fingers on one side and six on the other."

"All I want is five normal fingers on each hand," Nick said, wondering if all that candy had affected his friend's brain. "Make sure you put it on straight though. I don't want to end up with a backwards finger when this is all over."

"Hold steady now." Nick watched as Angelo stitched his finger in place like he was sewing a button back on. He could feel a slight poke as the needle went in and out of his flesh, but other than that there was no sensation at all.

Angelo took off his glasses and wiped sweat from his forehead. He tucked the needle and some extra line in his notebook. "I wouldn't try wiggling it or anything until you're human again."

"And don't pick your nose with it," Carter added. "It would suck to get it stuck up there."

"Thanks for the tip." Nick took the amulet out from the front of his shirt. "Guess it's time to finally take this off." All three boys stared at the gleaming red gem in the center. He'd sort of gotten used to wearing it, and although he was ready to stop being a zombie, part of him knew he would miss it. "Do you think I'm supposed to say something first?"

Angelo looked unsure. It was an expression Nick wasn't used to seeing on his friend's face. "I couldn't find anything about removing a cursed amulet in any of my books. I guess you'll have to try and see what happens."

Although his heart had slowed to nearly nothing, Nick thought he could feel it hammering in his chest. He gripped the amulet tightly in his left hand. Even after everything that had happened, there was a part of him that didn't want to take the chain off—as if the amulet itself was telling him to keep it on.

"Well, what are you waiting for?" Carter said.

"Give me a second!" Nick snapped. Nick's palm was

slick and the stone felt warm against his skin. What was wrong with him? Why couldn't he pull it off?

"Do you want me to help?" Angelo stepped toward him and Nick jerked backward.

"Are you okay?" Carter asked.

"Yeah," Nick muttered. "I just . . ." Just *what*? Did he want to stay a stinking creature with open sores and body parts falling off? In one swift motion he jerked the amulet over his head and pulled the chain from his neck.

All three boys sat silently, watching and waiting.

"How do you feel?" Carter asked.

Nick shrugged. "Okay, I guess." He looked at Angelo. "Am I . . . human?"

Angelo pressed a finger to the side of Nick's neck, frowning. After a moment, he put his ear to Nick's chest and listened. When he lifted his head, his expression was grim. "I think we have a bigger problem than we thought."

Nick ran a thumb across the base of his sewn-together pinky. "You're saying I'm stuck this way?"

Angelo bit his lower lip, flipping through the pages of his monster notebook over and over. "I'm saying I don't know."

"Maybe he just has to wait a while," Carter suggested, biting the end off a Tootsie Roll.

"Sure," Nick nodded, wanting to believe. He could afford to wait another day or two if he had to. That was a lot better than explaining to his parents that they had a zombie for a son and it was only a matter of time before he turned into a mindless, drooling freak, driven by an insatiable desire to consume human brain tissue.

"Possibly." Angelo nodded slowly. "Or maybe there's something we're missing. Maybe there's a way to turn you back. But the longer we wait, the harder it will become. I say we try everything we can think of. If nothing works, then we wait."

"Okay, that makes sense," Nick agreed. "But we can't do it here. I'm not grounded yet, though once my parents wake up, that could change. How about we each search for anything that might remove a curse and meet at the park in an hour?"

Sixty minutes later, Nick rode his bike up to the picnic tables beside the little playground at the center of Dinosaur Park. Clutched in his hand was a small brown bag. Carter was already there with a bag of his own. "What did you bring?" Nick asked, looking hopefully at the package.

Carter studied his feet. "Just, you know, some stuff. How about you?"

Nick leaned his bike against the table. "Stuff."

Unable to meet each other's eyes, the two boys waited for Angelo to arrive. If Carter's bag held anything similar to what Nick had brought, their only hope was Angelo. Fifteen minutes later, Angelo rode up with a thick book Nick thought he recognized from the library and a green bottle.

Nick read the label on the bottle. "Lemon juice?"

"You have something better?" Angelo asked, holding up his hands.

"No," Nick admitted. "Is that the book Mr. Blackham gave you?"

Angelo set the thick tome on the picnic table. "Yes. But let's try everything else first." He looked at Carter. "What did you come up with?"

Carter pulled out a small white plastic bottle.

"Acne cream?" Nick laughed.

"Hey," Carter said, his face turning red. "My big sister's skin looked ten times worse than yours before she started using this stuff. Of course she doesn't look all that much better now. But if it makes zits go away . . ."

"I guess it's worth a try," Nick said. He squeezed a

small puddle of the medicine into his palm and rubbed it across his face.

"Do you feel any different?' Angelo asked after a couple of minutes had passed.

Nick shook his head.

"What did you bring?" Carter asked, reaching for Nick's bag.

Nick wished he hadn't laughed at Carter earlier. He opened his sack and pulled out a metal spray can and a jar of lotion.

Carter held his stomach as he roared with laughter. "Spot remover and Bald-B-Gone?"

Nick scowled. "One makes spots go away and one is supposed to get rid of baldness. It was all I could find. Besides, it's not any dumber than zit cream."

That quieted Carter.

Nick already knew neither of them would work, but he sprayed some spot remover on the back of his neck and applied a little of the hair restorer to the top of his head. The three boys stood around, looking at the swings and slides that stood eerily empty at this time of the morning. "Nothing," Nick said when Carter finally peeked in his direction.

They both turned to Angelo, who held out the bottle of lemon juice. "This is supposed to clear up colds. But

my grandma swore it could cure anything."

Nick took the bottle. "What do I do with it?" From the look on Angelo's face he could tell it wasn't going to be good.

Angelo flipped through his notebook and studied the page, although Nick thought he might actually be using it as an excuse to keep from looking at him. "It says here, you, uh, put two drops of lemon juice in each of your nostrils."

Nick stumbled backward. "Are you kidding me? Do you have any idea how much that would sting?"

"Actually, by this point I doubt you'll feel anything at all. But you don't have to try it if you don't want to." Angelo rubbed the side of his face. "Who knows, maybe the spot remover will kick in."

Grumbling, Nick unscrewed the bottle and filled the lid with juice. "I think *you* should try it first," he muttered. But Angelo was right. He didn't have a lot of choices. Tilting back his head, he poured a little of the juice into each side of his nose. Angelo was right. The only thing he felt was a sort of gagging as the juice ran from his sinuses into his throat.

"Rut wow?" he said, trying to keep from inhaling.

"I think he's asking 'what now?'" Carter said.

Angelo referred to the notebook. "Stand on one

foot, and jump backward three times while repeating the words 'out, out, out.'"

Nick stared at him out of the corner of his eye, wondering if Angelo was pulling some kind of terrible prank. But his friend looked serious. A little at a time, he lifted his left foot into the air. With his muscles starting to deteriorate, his balance was bad enough. With his head tilted back and his eyes watering, it was almost impossible to stand on one foot, let alone jump.

"Out," he grunted, jumping backward. He almost fell, but by holding out his hands managed to catch himself. He began to sway. He was going to have to do this quick.

"Out." He jumped backward. He felt himself toppling over and jumped again.

"Out."

"Watch the table!" Carter yelled.

Nick's leg hit the corner of the picnic bench. He flailed his hands, trying to keep from falling. Angelo reached for his arm but missed. Like a big, awkward flamingo, he flapped, spun, and flew for two or three feet before smashing headfirst into the ground.

"Are you okay?" Carter ran toward him.

Angelo got there first and pulled him to his feet. He said something, but Nick couldn't make it out.

"What?"

Angelo held out his hand and moved to Nick's right side. "I said, I think you lost something."

Nick looked at what Angelo was holding. It was his left ear. "It fell off when you back-flipped over the picnic bench."

Carter skidded to a stop on the damp grass. He looked from Angelo to Nick and scratched the back of his neck. "If you don't want that, can I have it for a souvenir?"

Nick sat on the picnic table as Angelo sewed his ear back on. "How does it look?"

Carter made a square with his thumbs and fingers, like a photographer lining up a shot. "Has your nose always leaned to the left like that?"

"I'm not talking about my nose, you freakball," Nick growled. "I'm talking about my ear."

"Just trying to help." Carter wandered away, searching through his ever-diminishing candy supply.

"You look fine," Angelo said. "But we need to get this curse removed soon or you're going to be sewing body parts on faster than Carter eats candy."

"You don't need to tell me." Nick poked at his ear

with one finger. It seemed okay. He glanced at the book Angelo had carried to the park. "What's in that, anyway?"

Angelo picked up the heavy volume. The cover was made of something thick and pebbly that looked way too much like human skin for Nick's comfort. The title was written in a language he didn't recognize. *"Les malédictions et les remèdes,"* Nick read, stumbling over the words.

"It's French," Angelo said. "It means 'curses and cures.'"

Carter stepped in for a better look. "I didn't know you could read French."

"I can't," Angelo admitted. "At least, not much. And most of it's so old it's not even written in the kind of French they teach in school. But I've been using a French-English dictionary to figure most of it out."

"Does it say anything about zombie curses?" he asked.

"Sort of." Angelo opened the book to a page with a picture of a corpse climbing out of a grave.

"Cool!" Carter said, stepping closer to get a better look.

Nick examined the picture closely and shuddered. The creature looked like a skeleton with a thin coating

of peeling flesh. One of its legs was hanging by a thread and its left arm was completely gone. "Is this how I'm going to end up?"

"It's possible," Angelo said. "This doesn't talk specifically about zombies. But it does say the only way to remove a powerful voodoo curse is to make something called a mojo hand."

There was lots of writing on the page opposite the corpse and a drawing of what looked like a small bag. "If you already had this, why did you make me try all that other stuff?" Nick asked.

"I was hoping it wouldn't come this far." Angelo exhaled. He ran a finger along the words on the page. "I'm not sure I got the translation completely right. But from what I can tell, the mojo hand we need to make requires nine items. A broken ring, a voodoo doll's head, powdered bat, rat hair, human bone, the rotted flesh of a smoked pig, stench of death—whatever that is—a bloody dagger, and the ashes of an alchemist's handbook."

Nick stared at him. "Are you kidding me? Where would we get *any* of that?"

"It gets worse," Angelo said. "We have to combine all these items in a red flannel bag and read these words over a lit black candle at midnight in a cemetery." Carter

opened his mouth, but Angelo wasn't finished. "And all of this has to be completed within one week from the day the curse took effect."

"Wait, that would mean tonight," Carter said.

Nick wasn't sure he wanted to hear the answer, but he had to ask: "What happens if I miss the deadline?"

Angelo looked down at the book, his lips pressed tightly together, and tapped the picture of the walking corpse. "Then the curse becomes permanent."

Nick couldn't speak. His throat was too tight. Why had he ever gone into that cemetery in the first place? Why had his aunt been a voodoo queen? Why had his parents made him go to her funeral? There were lots of whys, but none of them mattered anymore. Becoming a zombie had seemed totally awesome at first. Now that it was permanent, he couldn't imagine anything worse. He was going to be a freak for the rest of his life—however long (or short) that might be.

Carter leaned forward and clapped his hands, startling both Angelo and Nick. He checked his watch. "Okay, it's almost nine now. That gives us fifteen hours to collect the ingredients and get to the cemetery."

"Are you kidding?" Nick blurted. "We can't get that stuff."

"So you're just going to give up?" Carter ran a hand across his spiky hair and shook his head. "We're the

Three Monsterteers, and I'm not letting any friend of mine stay undead if I can help it." He looked down at the list, trying to sound out the strange words. "Okay. I'll get the less preparation in powdered cheese swirls, sickly rat, and older day mort," he said, butchering the French words so badly even Nick cringed a little.

"Préparations en poudre chauve-souris, sèche de rat, and *odeur de mort,"* Angelo corrected. "You're going to find powdered bat, rat's hair, and the stench of death?"

Carter blinked but didn't look away. "Yes."

Angelo swallowed. "I guess I could try for the bloody dagger, the voodoo doll's head, and the human bone."

Nick looked from one of his friends to the other. This was crazy. But if his friends weren't going to quit, how could he? "All right," he said roughly. "That leaves me with the broken ring, the rotted flesh of a smoked pig, and the alchemist's handbook. I'll see if I can find a red flannel bag and a black candle, too." He put out his fist. Carter bumped it with his, and Angelo's made three. "We'll meet at the cemetery at eleven thirty."

"Eleven thirty," Angelo repeated.

"Eleven thirty." Carter grinned. "This is going to be awesome sauce."

Nick looked at the kitchen clock, clenching and unclenching his fists. It was after ten thirty and all he'd

been able to come up with was the black candle (left-over from his dad's fortieth birthday party), the red flannel bag (actually, it was a piece of his old flannel footie pajamas he'd stapled into a bag, but he figured that would have to work), and a plastic Oakland Raiders football ring he'd gotten from a gumball machine when he was ten. He still had to come up with the ashes of an alchemist's handbook and the rotted flesh of a smoked pig. And he had a little over an hour till midnight.

"You're up late," Mom said, walking into the kitchen from the living room, where she and Dad had been watching a movie. "Everything okay?" She reached out to feel Nick's forehead, but he pulled back. What would she do if she touched his skin and realized it was now nearly as cold as the inside of the refrigerator?

"Sure," Nick said, trying to smile. "I'm just trying to figure out a . . . school project."

"Why don't you tell me about this *project*? Maybe I can help." Mom folded her arms across her chest and Nick could tell she wasn't convinced. He frowned. How could he possibly tell her what he needed without giving everything away?

"It's sort of a science experiment," he said. "We're testing how long things take to break down. I was supposed to bring, uh, smoked pig's flesh."

Mom's forehead wrinkled and Nick was sure he was

busted. Then she laughed. "You mean sausage?"

Nick stared. "Sausage is smoked pig's flesh?"

She nodded. "Not completely. But there *is* smoked pork in lots of things. Sausage, ribs, baloney, ham, barbecue. Even some hot dogs, I think."

Nick had never considered that ordinary meat might have smoked pig's flesh in it. It was both exciting and kind of disgusting at the same time. "Do we have any of those things?"

Mom opened the fridge and then the freezer. "Sorry," she said, and Nick's heart dropped. "Your dad must have finished the sausage last week, and I used the last of the baloney in your lunch."

She ruffled his hair. "I can pick something up at the store tomorrow."

Tomorrow would be too late. And even if he could talk her into going to the store now, the meat would be fresh, not rotten like the ceremony called for. It was too late. He was doomed. "That's okay." He tried not to give away how horrible he felt. "I'm sure I can come up with something else."

As Nick began to shuffle out of the kitchen, Mom said, "Are you sure there's nothing you want to tell me? You've been in kind of a funk all week."

For a minute he considered telling her everything. It would be such a relief to turn this all over to a grown-up.

But what were the chances she'd believe him? And if she did, would she let him go off to the cemetery at midnight? By the time he'd convinced her he really was a zombie, it would be too late to do anything about it. He'd gotten himself into this and now he was going to have to live with it.

Besides, he couldn't keep stitching pieces of himself back together forever. It wouldn't be long before she figured it out on her own.

"I think I might be coming down with a cold or something," he said. "I'll go take a rest." He wandered into his room and collapsed onto his bed. He knew he needed to call his friends and tell them he'd failed. He just couldn't bring himself to do it.

A few minutes later Dad poked his head through the door. "Everything okay, young grasshopper? Your mom says you've been looking kind of blue. And for grasshoppers, that's lethal. Only cure is a frixleberry shake. You want me to whip one up for you before you go to sleep?"

"There's no such thing as a frixleberry," Nick muttered. He knew his dad was only trying to cheer him up. But there was nothing that could do that except for breaking his curse. "I'm just going to go to sleep." He rolled over and buried his face in his pillow. "Unless

you happen to know where I could find an alchemist's handbook."

"An alchemist's handbook?" Nick looked up to see his dad beaming. "Is that what you need? Why didn't you say so in the first place?"

Nick sat up as his dad disappeared into the hall and up the stairs. Was it really possible? Could his father really know where to find an alchemist's handbook? A minute later, his dad's footsteps came back down the stairs. He tossed a heavy book onto the bed. "College chemistry, to be precise. But as long ago as I took it, it might as well be alchemy."

Nick stared at the textbook. Would it work? It was better than anything else he could think of.

"I've also got an excellent treatise on out-of-date psychology and *Discovering the Wheel for Dummies* if you need those." Dad started out the door, then turned back. "You really should clean your room. Your mom's right. It smells like a chimp cage in here."

Nick wanted to tell his Dad he might as well get used to it, since he now had barely an hour to find a piece of rotted pig and complete the ceremony.

Dad picked up a brown bag by the door. He took a whiff and made a face. "Whew," he said, pulling out a plastic baggy. "This is part of the problem."

It was the lunch Nick's mom had given him a few days earlier. He'd offered it to Carter with no success. There were few kinds of food Carter would turn down. But one of them was . . .

Nick jumped off his bed. He ran across the room and snatched the bag from his dad's hand. In the warmth of his room the sandwich had quickly gone bad. Green mold spores covered the mayonnaise, the bread, and especially the—

"Baloney," he said. "Rotten baloney." He squeezed his dad as tight as he could. "You're the best."

Dad scratched the back of his head and shrugged. "College chemistry and a moldy sandwich. What more could a boy ask for?"

Nick lowered his head and pedaled as fast as he could, disappearing from the illuminated circle of one streetlamp and reappearing in the next as he raced along the black asphalt. He'd wasted more than fifteen minutes lying quietly in his bed, waiting for his parents to go to their room. If they tried to check on him and discovered he'd climbed out the window, he would be grounded for life. But he couldn't worry about that now.

By the time he reached the cemetery, it was 11:35 and the gate had long since been closed and locked. He spotted tire tracks in the cemetery grass and realized Angelo must have thrown his bike over the fence.

Nick did the same thing, although he could barely manage to get his bike over. Being careful not to catch his clothes on the metal spikes at the top of each pole, he climbed the fence and jumped to the damp grass. His aunt's *pot tet* and the amulet clinked against each other in his pocket. He followed the tracks between rows of ghostly white grave markers, and a minute later found Angelo standing between a pair of tall headstones.

"Where's Carter?" Nick asked, leaping off his bike.

Angelo shrugged. "No clue. I've been waiting here for more than fifteen minutes by myself. It was creepy." He looked over his shoulder. "I was starting to feel like there was someone spying on me." Something that sounded a little like a human voice floated on the night air, and both boys glanced nervously around.

Nick checked his watch. Time was getting short. "Sorry. I had a little trouble finding all the stuff. How did *you* do?"

Angelo picked up a black backpack by his feet and pulled out a pearl-handled dagger.

"Nice," Nick said, admiring the sharp silver blade. "Where'd you get that?"

"It's actually a letter opener. But the blood on the tip is real." Angelo held out a finger with a bandage wrapped around it.

Nick winced. "Ouch. Thanks, man." He took the dagger and dropped it into his bag.

"I was stumped on the human bone until I remembered the time I fell off my bike and broke my leg," Angelo said. Nick remembered. It had been a really bad break and Angelo had been on crutches for nearly three months.

Angelo took a small silver rod out of the backpack and held it up to the moonlight. It took Nick a moment to realize what it was. "They put this pin in my leg to hold the bones in place while they healed," Angelo said, turning the rod in his hand. "The doctor gave it to me after they took it out. If you put it under a microscope you can see tiny bits of bone on it. It's not much, but the book didn't say you had to have a certain amount."

It was brilliant. Nick began to think this might really happen—if Carter got there. He checked the time and saw there were now less than twenty minutes left.

Angelo dipped into his bag again and Nick was sure he was going to pull out a Barbie head or something like that. But when Angelo showed him the voodoo doll head, it looked just like something you'd see in one of those horror movies where people stick pins in a doll to get revenge on their enemies. "I made it myself," Angelo said. "There were detailed drawings in the library book."

As Nick stared into the tiny cloth face, with its black beads for eyes and a stitched mouth sewn into a seriously spooky smile, a shiver ran down his back. Did they understand what they were messing with here? They were just a couple of kids, standing in the middle of a cemetery at midnight, thinking about performing a ceremony from a book written before their parents were born—and maybe before their grandparents or even great-grandparents.

A cold wind blew his hair back from his face and something moved in the bushes to the left. Nick stared at Angelo. His friend looked just as scared as he was. Nick opened his mouth to say something, but before he could, a figure leaped out of the darkness. Torn clothes fluttered from its thin arms and legs and its face was matted with dirt and grass. Sure it was a corpse come to life, Nick backed away until a familiar voice said, "Thanks for nothing!"

"Carter?" Nick asked. "What happened to you?"

Carter rubbed his hands on the front of his shirt,

leaving green and brown smears. "I got stuck on the fence. I kept shouting for you guys, but you never came. Finally I had to rip my pants to get down." He turned around, revealing a hole in the back of his jeans with a pair of yellow smiley-face boxers showing through. "Once I got loose, I fell straight into a mud puddle."

"Sorry," Nick said. "We heard something, but we didn't know it was you."

Carter grunted. "You're going to owe me huge when this is all over. But we don't have time for that now." He reached into his pants pocket and took out a couple of long blond hairs. "Okay, here you go. I pulled these straight off my little sister's head."

Nick glanced at Angelo. "Um, didn't the book say the hairs of a *rat*?"

Carter nodded, handing the long strands to Nick. "Trust me. She is. Every time I do something wrong, she goes straight to my parents and rats on me."

Nick shrugged and tucked the hair into his flannel bag. If moldy baloney counted as rotted flesh of a smoked pig and his dad's chemistry book could be substituted for an alchemist's handbook, why couldn't Carter's little sister be a rat?

"Hurry up," Angelo said, rubbing his arms. The

wind was starting to pick up and the temperature was dropping.

"Okay, okay." Carter reached into his pocket again and pulled out a sock so stiff with sweat and dirt that it actually crackled as he waved it back and forth.

"Is that your sister's too?" Nick asked.

"No way," Carter said with a big grin. "Only my brother has feet *this* stinky."

As the horrible odor wafted across to him, Angelo plugged his nose. "That definitely counts as the stench of death to me."

Nick pinched the tip of the sock between his finger and thumb, holding it as far away from him as he could before dropping it into the bag.

"And last of all . . ." Carter dug into his pocket and pulled out a handful of something powdery and white.

"Is that really powdered bat?" Angelo asked, adjusting his glasses as he studied the pale substance.

Nick leaned forward and sniffed. "It smells like . . . sawdust."

"It is." Carter laughed. "I thought I was going to be stuck until I realized it didn't say what *kind* of bat it had to be."

"A baseball bat!" Nick said, laughing too.

Carter nodded and dropped the sawdust into the bag. "I sanded it off myself with my dad's belt sander."

Now it was Nick's turn. He snapped the plastic Raiders ring in half and dropped it in. "The broken ring." Next he put in the piece of moldy baloney, explaining what he had learned from his mother about smoked pork. Last of all, he lit a match and burned a page from his father's old chemistry book, sprinkling the ashes into the bag. "Well, I guess this is it."

Angelo and Carter nodded silently, their faces pale in the silvery moonlight.

Nick took the black birthday candle out of his jacket pocket and stuck it in the ground, close to a headstone to block the wind.

"It's not very big," Carter whispered.

Angelo took the ancient book from his backpack and opened it to the right page. "We'll have to read fast before it burns out."

With shaking fingers, Nick tried to light another match. The first two times he failed. Finally, on his third try, the match flared to life and he held the wavering flame to the candle's wick.

"Hold the bag over the flame," Angelo said. "And repeat exactly what I say. We don't have time to do this twice."

Nick checked his watch. The minute hand was four marks away from midnight. The second hand seemed to be racing much too fast.

"Avec cette bougie noir," Angelo read, his voice soft and trembling.

"Avec cette bougie noir," Nick repeated, trying to say the words the same way Angelo did.

"Je supplie cette malédiction de s'écarter." At Angelo's words the wind began to howl and Nick had to raise his voice to be heard over it. Strangely, the candle flame didn't flicker at all. If anything, it seemed to burn brighter.

Nick had no idea what Angelo was saying as he read line after line from the book. But something was obviously happening. The night grew dark around him as if a giant hand had covered the moon. Icy wind ripped at his face. The ground beneath his feet started to tremble.

Something caught his eye and he turned to see a white shape rise from a grave a few feet to his left. "What is that?" he yelled, drawing back.

Carter and Angelo followed his gaze, but neither of them appeared to see what he was seeing. "What's what?" Carter yelled. His voice seemed far away even though he was standing right beside Nick. Another shape rose from the grave to his left and a pair of hungry eyes glared at him from a face that appeared to be made completely of smoke. Another of the transparent

shapes rose out of the ground, and another.

"Ghosts!" he yelled. "Everywhere. Can't you see them?"

Angelo shook his head. "It must be because you're undead. Ignore them and keep repeating the words."

Nick tried to ignore the shapes coming closer and closer, focusing on the words Angelo was reading.

"Hurry!" Carter screamed. "We're out of time."

Nick looked at his watch and had a sudden sense of déjà vu. It was 11:59, and the second hand was ten spaces from the top, just like it had been in the cemetery behind his aunt's house. Only then he'd been about to become a zombie. Now he was trying to stop being one.

Click. Nine. *Click.* Eight. "Last line," Angelo said. Holding the book close to his face, he read, *"Retournez ma vie à moi."*

Nick gulped. The ghosts were right on top of him now and he didn't dare meet their gazes. *"Retournez ma vie à—"*

As Nick was about to repeat the last word, something soft and black brushed past his leg and snuffed out the candle's flame. The second hand on his watch jumped forward and the minute hand clicked to midnight. All around him the wind stopped and the sky cleared. He looked down to see a black cat casually licking its paw.

It was too late. He'd missed the deadline. He was going to be a zombie forever.

"What happened?" Angelo asked, looking up from his book.

"It was that stupid cat," Carter said. "It put out the candle on purpose. I saw it." He pulled back his foot to kick, but the black cat jumped gracefully out of reach, staring at him with its green eyes as though asking, "Is that really necessary?"

"Maybe we can try again," Nick said. But even as he was saying it, he knew it was no good.

Angelo slammed the book shut and hung his head. "It's too late. Can't you feel it? I actually think the ceremony was working. But the energy is gone now."

Nick glared at the black cat sitting a few feet away.

It was the same one he'd seen watching him a couple of days earlier on his way to school, he was sure of it. And it still reminded him of another cat. One he'd seen somewhere before. He just couldn't quite . . .

"Excuse me," an odd-sounding voice said. Nick turned around, ready to tell Carter this was no time for joking. Instead he found a man looking at him with a pleased grin on his round face. The man was wearing an old-fashioned suit and holding a hat with a curved top in his hands. Nick took a quick step backward. He could see right through the man's body.

"I hate to trouble you," the man said, turning his hat around and around in his hands. "But I couldn't help overhearing you earlier, talking about a baloney sandwich."

"S-sandwich?" Nick stuttered. Carter and Angelo looked at him as if he'd suddenly gone crazy.

"I can't believe you're hungry at a time like this," Carter said. "But since you brought it up, I guess I could eat something too."

"Yes. Well, I was just wondering if you might happen to have a hot pastrami?" the see-through man asked Nick. He spoke with a stiff-sounding accent, his lips barely moving with each word. "On dark rye with spicy mustard and perhaps a dill pickle or two?" The

man rubbed his transparent stomach with a transparent hand.

Nick pointed toward the man. "There's a g-ghost," he whispered. "Right there. Can't you see him?"

"A ghost?" Angelo shoved the book into his backpack and grabbed his monster notebook. "What does it want?"

Nick clutched his hands together, trying to keep from all out panic. "I think he wants a pastrami sandwich."

"Where is it?" Carter asked, poking his hand right through the ghost's rather large belly.

Angelo scribbled quickly in his notebook. "Can ghosts eat food?"

"What? You want me to *ask* it?" Nick rolled his eyes.

Angelo nodded. "This could be important information in the study of parapsychology."

Nick looked at the ghost, wondering if this whole thing might be in his head—if turning into a zombie had finally driven him bonkers. "Can you . . . *eat* a sandwich?"

The ghost sighed mournfully. "No. And it's the most terrible thing. But if I concentrate hard enough, I think I might manage to smell it a little. Oh, how I love the aroma of well-cured pastrami."

Another ghost edged up on Nick's left. This one was

a tall man with a bushy mustache on his narrow face. "If it's not too much trouble," the ghost asked, "could you possibly find me some shoes?" The ghost wriggled his toes and Nick saw he was only wearing a pair of ragged socks. "I was buried without my shoes on and my feet are simply frigid."

"Go away, Stenson," the fat ghost with the hat cried, glaring at the ghost with no shoes. "I found him first."

"You're nothing but a greedy pig, Alabaster," the thin ghost wailed. "You were in life and you are in death."

"What's it saying?" Angelo asked.

Nick rubbed the side of his face. "There are two of them now. They're fighting over shoes and sandwiches."

"Aren't you the handsome one?" a woman's voice said, and Nick turned to find a beautiful lady standing to his left. She was wearing a long, flowing white dress and holding a white umbrella. Like the two men, she also seemed to be made of nothing more substantial than fog.

"I, uh, well . . ." Nick stammered as the woman dropped her chin and gave him a wink. She reached out to touch Nick's arm and her fingers went right through him. Tendrils of icy cold pierced his flesh where her hand had gone in.

"What's happening? What's happening?" Angelo called, looking around as if he might be able to spot one of the ghosts himself. "Tell me everything you see. I should have brought my EMF meter."

"If I could just ask for one teensy-weensy favor," the woman said, twirling a lock of hair around one finger. Nick felt his face getting hot—or at least hotter than normal. "There's this man in the next cemetery over who—"

The two arguing men, realizing someone had taken their place, turned on the woman. "Leave the boy alone, Veronica, he's ours!" shouted the one called Alabaster.

"Be quiet, you buffoons," she snarled.

Other ghosts, noticing the commotion, began drifting toward Nick. Each of them had a request of their own.

"My money."

"My baby."

"My prize turkey."

"Come on," Nick said, backing away. "We have to get out of here." He dropped the flannel bag and grabbed his bike.

"But I haven't finished taking notes," Angelo said. "If I could just have you ask a few more questions."

"I'm not asking anything." The ghosts were all

looking at him now and none of them seemed happy that he was thinking of leaving. A low murmuring of disapproval quickly grew to a steady growl. Nick jumped on his bike and Carter climbed on behind him. A lumpy-looking man with a scar across the center of his face raised a ghostly shovel over his head and lunged forward. Nick closed his eyes and rammed his bike straight through him. A sensation like hundreds of icy needles poked at every inch of his exposed skin.

"What was that?" Carter yelled. "It felt like we just went through a cloud."

Nick shook his head. There was no time to explain. Not daring to look back, he pedaled toward the edge of the cemetery. As soon as he reached the fence, he jumped off his bike and heaved it over the top.

"Give me a boost," Carter said, clutching the bars.

Nick grabbed Carter's legs and immediately got an eyeful of bright yellow boxers. "Get your butt out of my face," he grunted, pushing and turning his head.

Carter giggled and shook his rear. "You're just lucky I'm too scared to let one rip."

As Carter leaped down to the other side, Nick risked a glance over his shoulder. There were hundreds of ghosts now, all heading in his direction. He grabbed the metal bars and vaulted himself over the

top like a monkey escaping from a cage full of tigers.

"Are they still coming?" Carter yelled as Nick hit the ground and rolled to his feet.

Nick spun around. The ghosts had stopped a hundred feet or so from the fence and were standing in a long line watching him with unhappy expressions on their shimmering faces. He shook his head. "I don't think they can leave the cemetery."

A minute later Angelo appeared wearing his backpack and riding his bike. He barreled through the ghosts, but if they could see him at all, they paid no attention.

"I can't believe you ran away," Angelo complained as he climbed over the fence. "Do you have any idea how many people have tried to communicate with spirits of the dead? This is the opportunity of a lifetime."

Nick scowled. "It wasn't *you* they were fighting over like a pack of hungry dogs trying to rip the last piece of meat from the bone. When *you* get turned into a zombie for the rest of your life, you can talk to them all you want."

Angelo lowered his eyes. "I'm sorry. I wasn't thinking." He kicked at a pile of grass clippings. "This is my fault. I should have gone to the library sooner."

"It's not your fault," Nick said. "It's not any of our faults. We did everything we could. If there's anyone

to blame, it's my aunt Lenore. She must have known the amulet was behind her house and what it could do. Why didn't she destroy it?"

"Maybe she couldn't," Angelo said.

"Hey." Carter pointed down the street. "There's the cat that blew out the candle."

The black cat, standing in the light of a street lamp, looked straight at the three boys, meowed, and turned in a circle.

Carter picked up a rock and drew back his arm. The cat flinched as if getting ready to run. But Nick grabbed Carter's arm. "Hang on," he said. "I've seen that cat before. It looks just like the cat that led me into the cemetery behind my aunt's house. The cemetery where I found the amulet."

"There's no way a cat came all the way from Louisiana by itself," Angelo said.

Nick knew he was right. But he was almost sure it was the same cat. The perfectly black fur, the knowing green eyes—even the sound of its meow was familiar.

"Meow, meow," the cat said. It walked in a circle again, waved a paw in the boys' direction, then turned and started down the street.

Nick looked from Carter to Angelo. "I think it wants us to follow it."

Nick, Angelo, and Carter rode their bikes through the night, following the cat who, despite the boys' best efforts to catch up, managed to stay far enough ahead to lead them without disappearing completely.

"Where do you think it's going?" Carter asked, his nearly empty Halloween bag swinging back and forth from his handlebars.

Nick had no idea. They'd gone from the residential section of town to an area of small businesses and shops he wasn't familiar with. "I just hope we get there soon. I didn't tell my parents I was leaving. If they find out, I'm a goner."

"My mom's out of town visiting my sister," Angelo

said. He had the longest legs and easily stayed at the front of the group.

Carter, who was pedaling like crazy to keep up, huffed and puffed. "I . . . told my parents . . . I was . . . spending the night at . . . Angelo's house. I think . . . they were glad . . . to . . . see me go . . . after I . . . pulled out my . . . sister's hair."

The cat stopped at the corner of a closed bakery, glanced back to make sure the boys were still following, then darted around the brick wall. When they reached the spot they'd last seen the cat, the boys stopped their bikes and peered into a dark alley.

"Where did it go?" Angelo said. With tall buildings on either side blocking the moon and no lights in the alley itself, it was impossible to see more than a few feet ahead.

Nick wished he still had his matches, but he'd dropped them in the cemetery along with everything else. "Come on," he said, getting off his bike and pushing it. "But stay close."

As he walked deeper into the alleyway, Nick's eyes began to adjust. He could make out a couple of trash cans, a stack of old newspapers, and several broken bottles. But there was no sign of the cat anywhere.

"It's like it vanished," Angelo said.

Carter shuffled along the grungy street, his head swinging left and right with each step. "I do *not* like this. Maybe we should turn around."

"Wait," Nick said. There was something at the end of the alley. When he got close enough, he could see it was a door. A sign on the front read GRANDMA ELISHEBA'S: PALM READING, FORTUNE-TELLING, LOVE POTIONS, AND CHARMS. "Why would the cat bring us here?"

"It's got to be closed," Angelo said.

Nick agreed. But where had the cat gone? "It's not like it could open the door by itself," he said.

"I don't care if it's closed or not," Carter said. "I'm not going in there."

Nick wasn't sure they had much choice. It was either try the door or turn around and admit defeat. He reached for the tarnished brass knob. Before he could touch it, the door swung open by itself, a square of feeble light shining into the alley. A voice said, "I be waiting for you."

"It's a ghost," Carter said, his hands shaking so badly his entire bicycle rattled.

"Not if *you* can hear it," Nick said.

Lying on the floor just inside the doorway was an old broom. Nick remembered seeing a broom lying just the same way at the top of the stairs in his aunt's

house. He reached down to pick it up, but the voice spoke again. "You best not be touching that or trying to cross over—*not in your condition*."

"What do you know about my condition?" Nick asked. He couldn't see much in the room beyond, other than a few flickering candles.

The voice laughed and Nick had the impression of great age. An old woman maybe? "Oh, I know all 'bout your problem," the voice said. "How you be getting it in the first place. More important, *why*."

Nick glanced to his left, where Angelo was rubbing a finger over his lower lip. "Some cultures believe a crossed broom protects against evil spirits and the undead," Angelo whispered. He leaned down and carefully picked up the broom.

"He be a smart boy, that one." The voice cackled and Nick imagined a witch waiting for them just inside. Wondering if he was making a big mistake, he stepped through the doorway. Angelo followed him, and Carter came through last, dragging his feet with each step.

Inside, the air was strong with the smell of spices and candle wax. There was another less pleasant smell underneath the spicy aroma that made Nick think of a butcher's shop. Near the back of the room, a figure sat at a small round table. As Nick moved closer, he could

see it was a woman. Her face was lined with wrinkles and her long hair was almost completely white. Her left hand lay flat on the table while her right stroked the back of the cat that had led them there.

Nick squinted into the darkness. "I know you."

The woman pursed her lips. "Do you now?"

Nick took a step closer. "You were at my aunt's funeral."

The woman laughed, her voice dry and dusty-sounding. "You be observant."

A few things began to add up. If this woman was at the funeral and this was her cat . . . "You're the one who left me the note saying to trust the cat. You tricked me into following him into the cemetery."

"Her," the old woman said, unaffected by Nick's accusation. She rubbed her cat under the chin. "This is my Isabelle. And yes, she led you into the cemetery."

"I don't care what your cat's name is!" Nick's entire body began to shake as anger boiled up inside him. "It's your fault I found the amulet. It's your fault I'm . . . the way I am."

"A *zombie*?" The woman continued to comb her hand through her cat's thick black fur, the rings on her fingers flashing blue, red, and gold in the reflected candlelight. "Perhaps I can help with that."

"Don't trust her," Carter said, pushing forward. "She wants you to stay a zombie. That's why she had her cat ruin the ceremony."

The woman's dark eyes glittered.

"He's right," Nick said. "Let's get out of here. I don't need you." He started to turn away, but the woman's voice pulled him back.

"Oh, but you do," she said. "I be the only one who knows how the curse be broken."

"It's too late for that," Angelo said.

The old woman waved her hand, sending the candles flickering. "You think that nonsense you were doing in the cemetery tonight be breaking a curse this strong? Much more likely it kill. I probably be saving your life."

Nick felt something cold and loose inside of him. Could she be telling the truth? Was it possible he'd nearly died tonight? He glanced at his friends. Neither of them looked any surer than he felt. True, they all loved monsters and monster movies, but this kind of thing was way over their heads.

"You can break the curse?" he asked.

The old woman cackled so hard she began to cough. She pressed her hand to her mouth, her body shaking with deep, bone-rattling hacks, as though choking on

something wet. When she finally got her voice back, she sounded tired. "'Course not."

Nick's disappointment was so strong he could taste it. "If you can't cure me, then why did you bring us here?"

The woman glared at him. "You listen to Grandma Elisheba. And listen well. No one break that curse o' yours 'cept the one who created it in the first place. You want it broken, you got to go to the one himself. The Zombie King."

Nick swallowed so hard everyone in the room could hear it. "The *king*?"

The woman laughed again. "You hear of him, yes?"

Nick nodded. "My aunt wrote about a king in her journal."

Grandma Elisheba's face darkened. "You read her journal?"

Nick nodded. "Most of it was burned, but she said this king was a bokor—that he was trying to get back at her from the grave. She killed him?"

Grandma Elisheba shook her head violently. "The Zombie King not dead. Not that one. Only trapped." She pointed a trembling finger at Nick. "He wants that amulet of yours bad. He knows you come to your aunt's funeral. And he knows you be the only one can enter

that crypt. If you don't go on your own, he make you go. You not be surviving that."

That must have been the treasure his aunt had been writing about. Nick thought for a moment. "So you're saying my amulet belongs to this Zombie King. And that if I hadn't gotten it on my own, he would have forced me to get it and killed me?"

The old woman nodded. "That be why I follow you that night. I push you into the crypt to save you from the Zombie King."

Something about the old woman's words didn't completely add up, but Nick couldn't quite figure it out. "Thanks for saving my life, I guess. If I give it back to him, it will break my curse?"

She nodded again.

It did make a kind of strange sense. Although Nick still wasn't sure he trusted this woman. Then he remembered something else from the journal. "You're the E my grandmother wrote about."

The old woman stared at him, her face unreadable.

"She said that you'd given in. That you wanted the amulet. And something about a girl."

"I know nothing 'bout that," Elisheba said. "I want nothing to do with that cursed t'ing. Take my advice or don't."

Nick still had a bad feeling. If she'd really been trying to save his life, why hadn't she told him about the amulet in the first place instead of tricking him into putting it on? Then again, he'd didn't have any other options left. "You can lead us to this Zombie King?"

Grandma Elisheba burst into startled laughter again, waving both of her hands in his direction. "Don't you listen, child? You don't walk to the Zombie King and knock on his door. He be trapped in his own realm—somewhere twixt here and the underworld."

"Then what's the point?" Nick slapped his hand to his forehead in frustration and thought he felt another of his fingers loosen. "Why tell us about this Zombie King dude if you can't take us to him?"

"I cannot," the woman said with a sly smile. "But I be knowing one who can. You must speak to the lord of the graveyard. The Baron Cemetier."

"I still don't trust that crazy old lady," Carter said.

Nick rocked his bike back and forth, unable to keep still. "I don't either."

The three boys were huddled outside the cemetery fence near the spot where Carter had ripped his pants earlier that night. Isabelle, the black cat, circled impatiently around them, but they ignored her.

Nick looked at the ghosts gathered on the other side of the fence. They had appeared shortly after he and his friends arrived, as though drawn by a magnet. "You really think that stuff will keep them away?" he asked, reaching for the small silk bag Grandma Elisheba had given them.

Angelo pulled it out of Nick's reach. "Don't forget what she said. The undead aren't supposed to touch this." He bounced the bag in his hand. "I've read about black salt. It's made by combining cauldron scrapings with regular salt. It's supposed to create a protective barrier. There was something else . . ." He rubbed his forehead as though willing the contents of his brain to come forward. "I can't remember what."

The cat stopped and cocked its head almost as if it understood their conversation.

Nick felt extremely nervous about what they were doing and the woman who had sent them there. "This could be dangerous," he said. "There's no reason for you guys to take the risk. I'm the only one who needs to see the Zombie King."

"You think I'd let you go without me?" Angelo said. "This is the chance of a lifetime. If you're going, I'm going."

"I'm not gonna lie," Carter said, rubbing his hands across his mud-stained pants. "I'm so scared I think I might hurl. But I'm not letting you do this alone. We're the Three Monsterteers."

Nick knew he had the best friends ever. "Okay," he said, throwing down his bike. "If we're going to do this, let's go."

Angelo and Nick gripped Carter's feet, boosting him over the fence. As they lifted him, a smell even more disgusting than Carter's sweat socks filled the air. Nick wondered if it might be coming from the cemetery itself, until Carter giggled and waved a hand behind his rear. "Uh, sorry about that."

Angelo grimaced. "That's just gross, man."

Nick laughed. Some things would never change. "I can't believe you're still hauling around that candy bag," he said as he and Angelo climbed into the cemetery.

"I get hungry," Carter said. "Especially when I get scared. Not that there's much good stuff left." He stared sadly into the bag. "Seriously, what kind of demented person hands out Bit-O-Honeys?"

Just as Grandma Elisheba had promised, as soon as the boys were inside the fence, the black cat slid between the metal bars and led the way deeper into the cemetery. The old woman appeared to be right about the black salt as well. Although the ghosts followed the boys as they wound around headstones and between graves, none of them came close enough to cause any trouble.

"Who do you think this Baron Cemetier is?" Nick whispered to Angelo. Even though there was no one around to overhear him except for the ghosts, he found

himself keeping his voice low. "Maybe he works here or something?"

Angelo took off his glasses and rubbed them on the front of his shirt. "She said to be sure to pour a closed circle of black salt around us before summoning him," he said. "Last time I checked, you don't have to protect yourself from cemetery workers."

Lost in thought, Nick, Angelo, and Carter trooped silently behind the cat until at last it stopped before a crackled angel statue that looked like a strong wind might blow it to pieces. As soon as the cat reached the statue, it leaped onto the stone pedestal and curled up at the base of the angel.

"I guess this is the place," Nick said.

"Meow." The cat licked a paw and scrubbed the back of its head.

Carter frowned. "I don't like that cat. It always looks like it's laughing at us."

"Squeeze together," Angelo said. "There's not much of this salt, and Grandma Elisheba said we all have to stand completely inside the circle." Holding the silk bag so only a few dark crystals could spill out at a time, Angelo carefully poured a circle in the short grass. By the time he had finished, the bag was nearly empty.

"Doesn't look like much," Carter said when the circle was complete.

Nick had to agree. If the Baron Cemetier was some kind of *monster*, he didn't like the idea of being protected by nothing more than a line of salt so thin it was nearly impossible to see in the dark night.

"It will have to do," Angelo said. He tucked the bag into his pocket and stepped inside the circle. There was barely enough room to stand side by side.

"Would you like me to do the summoning?" Angelo asked.

Nick shook his head. Compared to the elaborate ceremony required to make the mojo hand, summoning the Baron was nothing. Still, he found his voice trembling when he opened his mouth and said, "Baron Cemetier, come forth. Baron Cemetier, come forth. Baron Cemetier, come forth."

The last word had barely left his lips when the angel began shaking violently. Bits of stone flaked off the statue, peppering the cat's fur.

"I don't see any—" Nick started to say. The rest of his words froze in his mouth. A second before, he had been looking at a row of headstones in the distance. Now his view was blocked by an impossibly tall figure in black pants, a long black suit coat that came nearly to its knees, and a tall black hat with a red feather sticking

up out of the band.

The figure was facing away from them, and for a moment it didn't seem aware they were even there. Then, slowly, it turned. A man, tall enough to be an NBA basketball player, gripped a long silver blade with a white handle. His face was covered with shaving cream, as though he had been standing before the bathroom mirror a moment before. But what was so terrifying that Nick found himself pressing tightly against his friends, was that beneath the open coat of its tuxedo jacket, the creature was nothing but bones. The hand clutching the straight razor didn't have a single shred of flesh on its fingers. And the eyes staring at them from above the shaving cream were really just empty sockets.

"Well, well, what do we have here?" the skeleton said, wiping the shaving cream from its razor on one of its pant legs.

Nick tried to speak, but his tongue refused to unstick itself from the roof of his mouth.

"A-a-are y-you the B-baron C-c-c-c . . ." Angelo's voice was shaking so badly, he couldn't get out the last word, but Nick thought the very fact that he'd even tried was the bravest thing he'd ever seen.

"I am the Baron Cemetier, also known as Baron Samedi, Baron La Croix, and Lord of the Graveyard."

Samedi, Nick thought. *Where have I heard that name before?*

The skeleton's teeth widened a little in what Nick thought might have been a grin. It ran a bone hand over its face and the shaving cream vanished, leaving a gleaming white skull behind. "You know who I am, but I'm afraid I haven't made your acquaintance." It closed the straight razor with a wicked snap, tucked it inside its jacket pocket, and held out a hand.

Despite his terror, Nick found himself drawn forward, his hand rising to meet the Baron's skeletal grip. Before he could take a step toward the creature, a pair of hands grabbed him from behind.

"Careful," Angelo said.

Nick looked down. His foot hovered just above the thin line of the black circle.

The Baron Cemetier roared with laughter, his jawbones clicking against each other with a horrifying *tick-tick-tick.* A shiny black beetle dropped from between the skeleton's teeth and scurried into the grass.

"Someone has taught you well," the Baron said. Despite showing no sign of a tongue, throat, or larynx, his voice was deep and full. "However, if you are too rude to shake my hand, I'm afraid I have other business to attend to."

"Wait!" Nick called as the Baron began to turn away

from him. The empty black sockets fixed once more on his face, and he felt the spit in his mouth turn to dust. "We, that is, *I,* need you to help me find the Zombie King."

"We *all* do," Carter said, clutching the sleeve of Nick's jacket so tightly his fingers were white. "We're in this together."

"That's right," Angelo said, standing shoulder to shoulder with Nick.

The skull swung its gaze slowly across the boys, taking each of them in, one at a time. "The *Zombie King,*" the Baron said. He pointed a long white finger bone directly at Nick and Nick felt his insides turn to ice. "Do you three children have any idea what you are asking? The Zombie King is far more dangerous than you can imagine."

Nick reached into his pocket, brushing his finger over his aunt's gold *pot tet* before pulling out the amulet. "I need to return this to him."

The Baron's head snapped around at the sight of the glimmering red stone. "Let me see that."

"See with your eyes, not your hands," Carter said. Under his breath he whispered, "If you even have any eyes."

The Baron's mouth slammed shut, his teeth grinding together like rocks in a blender. "Give it to me and I

will see that the Zombie King gets it."

Nick shook his head. "We have to give it to him ourselves." Isabelle purred loudly and Nick got the impression that the cat was telling him he was doing well.

When the Baron spoke again, his voice was smooth and eerily calm. "So you wish to meet the Zombie King on your own, hmm? Very well. But don't say I didn't warn you."

"You'll take us there?" Nick asked.

The skeleton reached up and ran its hard white fingers over the feather in its hat. "For a price. What do you offer me in trade?"

Nick, Angelo, and Carter looked at each other in surprise. The old woman hadn't said anything about a price. Nick checked his pockets. The only thing in them was the metal bottle, and he couldn't give away his great-aunt's spirit. Except for his monster notebook, Angelo had left everything in his pack on the other side of the fence. They didn't even have their bikes, not that Nick could imagine a skeleton wanting those.

"We don't have anything to trade," Nick said.

"Then I'm afraid I can't help you." With a flash, the Baron disappeared, taking with him all hope of breaking Nick's curse.

"Hang on!" Carter dug into his pockets and pulled out a handful of change. He quickly sorted through the coins. "I've got a dollar and thirty-two cents. Although I think this quarter is actually Canadian."

The air around where the Baron had disappeared wavered ever so slightly. "I have no need of mortal currency," his disembodied voice said.

Angelo took off his watch. "This works up to fifty feet underwater."

"Junk," the voice said.

Nick thought furiously. *Samedi.* Why was that name so familiar? Then he remembered. The book on his aunt's desk—the one he'd been reading before the cat scared him. There had been something in it about a skeleton named Samedi. It said he had . . .

"Your trick-or-treat bag," he said, spinning around to look at Carter. "Do you still have it?"

Carter glanced down at his plastic bag, hanging limp and nearly empty. "You want a piece of candy? I thought you didn't like it now."

"Not me," Nick said. *"Him."* He pointed at the spot where the Baron Cemetier had been. "My aunt had a book in her basement. It said Samedi has an insatiable sweet tooth. Offer him some of the candy from your bag."

"Candy?" The air wavered again, and like a film coming slowly into focus, the Baron Cemetier reappeared. "Sweets?"

"Sure." Carter nodded, catching on. "Really *sweet* sweets. I, um, saved the best for last."

The Baron solidified and leaned toward the boys. "Show me."

Carter dug around the bottom of his Halloween bag. He pulled out several empty candy wrappers before finding a roll of Necco Wafers. "These are awesome. Best candy ever."

Nick smiled, knowing Carter hated Necco wafers and tried to trade them to his younger sisters for whatever he could get.

The Baron held out his hand and Carter tossed him the candy, making sure not to leave the circle. The skeleton caught the roll. He unwrapped the plastic and placed a wafer into his mouth.

"Bland," he said a second later. "What else do you possess?"

Carter fished around in the bag again and brought out a vanilla Tootsie Roll.

The Baron waved it away before Carter could even offer it to him. "Clearly inferior."

Carter pulled out a half-eaten caramel corn ball, but Nick shook his head. "It's all garbage," Carter whispered. "I finished the good stuff days ago."

"Hey, what's this?" Angelo reached into the bag and pulled out a miniature Snickers.

Carter grabbed the candy bar. "I was saving that."

Angelo glared at him.

"Fine!" Carter huffed. He held out the candy. "Here. It's chocolate, nougat, and peanuts."

The Baron shook his head. "Nuts hurt my teeth."

"There's nothing else," Carter said. He turned over the bag and dumped the last of his candy onto the ground. Nick had no idea there was so much tasteless candy in existence. Stale gummy bears, wax lips, black licorice chews, two sucked-on jawbreakers, three

Bit-O-Honeys, and an oatmeal-raisin bar.

"There," the Baron called, pointing to the ground near the edge of the circle. "What are those?"

Nick followed his gaze. The only things he saw were a few candy corns. "*These?*" he asked, picking up the orange, yellow, and white kernels.

"Yes!" The skeleton chomped its teeth excitedly. "I've never seen sweets quite like those before. They're so . . . *colorful.*"

Carter rolled his eyes and took the candy from Nick. "You have excellent taste."

The Baron snapped his hands open and closed, finger bones rattling. Carter tossed him the candy corns.

The Baron Cemetier caught the candies in midair and, like a gourmet sampling a rare dish, delicately placed one of them into his mouth. He nodded his head. "Yes-s-s." He popped his jaws open and closed, as if he were smacking his nonexistent lips. "This is simply . . . scrumptious."

Who would have guessed that a skeleton could like candy? And even weirder, that candy corn would be his favorite? As far as Nick was concerned, candy corns were like black jelly beans at Easter. You either ate them last, when you had nothing left, or found one of the few kids that liked them and traded them away. He

watched as the skeleton put another candy corn in his mouth. "So you'll take us to the Zombie King?"

The Baron held up one finger as he ate another candy corn. Then another. And finally the last one. "More," he said, holding out a hard white palm.

"That's it," Carter said. "You ate them all."

The skeleton turned its hollow eye sockets in his direction. "I *will* have more."

Carter gulped, shrinking under the Baron's withering stare. "There *are* no more."

The space around the Baron Cemetier darkened and the skeleton grew taller and taller, until the top of its hat was nearly even with the treetops. Although there were no clouds in the sky, lightning flashed and the ground rumbled. "I am the *Lord of the Graveyard.* You will obey me or you will never leave here alive!"

Angelo shook his head silently. What could they do? Carter knelt to the ground, sorting through empty wrappers and spilled Necco Wafers. But there had only been a few candy corns to begin with and it was clear the skeleton had eaten them all.

Isabelle, who had been watching everything from her perch on the stone pedestal, leaped to the ground. Nick thought the cat was trying to escape, until she pounced on something in the grass and batted it to him.

He reached down and picked up a candy corn.

A second later the cat discovered another, and another. Soon Nick held all five candies again. "Where did these come from?" he asked, wondering if the cat was somehow magic.

Angelo's normally serious face broke into a knowing smile. "The Baron is a skeleton. He doesn't have a throat or stomach. The candies fell right through him."

Nick beamed. Of course! "Here," he said, holding open his palm. "Have some more."

The Baron shrank to his normal size and the lightning disappeared from the sky. Nick threw him the candies and the Lord of the Graveyard ate them one by one. Every time he placed a candy corn into his mouth, it dropped straight through his body—occasionally bouncing off a rib or a long, pale leg bone. As the candies hit the ground, Isabelle found them and batted them back to Nick.

Nick continued tossing the candies to the Baron, wondering if a skeleton could ever get full since it had nothing to fill. At last though, the Baron placed a final candy between his perfect white teeth and sighed. "I couldn't eat one more bite," he groaned, rubbing the spot where his stomach would have been if he had one.

Nick sighed too. It had begun to feel like they would

be here all night. "*Now* will you send us to the Zombie King?"

The Baron brushed a bit of dust from one of his sleeves, took off his top hat, and straightened the jaunty red feather. "Are you sure that's what you want? I can take you to the Zombie King's realm, but you'll have to find your own way out."

Something in the skeleton's voice brought goose bumps to the backs of Nick's arms. "You still want to do this?" he whispered. Both of his friends nodded, although Carter's chin trembled visibly.

"Very well." The Baron Cemetier lifted his arms wide. The sleeves of his coat flapped like the wings of a huge bat. He opened his mouth and said something Nick couldn't understand. A cold wind raced across the graveyard. All around the cemetery bits of dirt and grass exploded from the ground.

The ghosts, who had been watching from a safe distance, disappeared back into their graves. The earth tilted under Nick's feet and he stumbled toward the edge of the circle. With a crack of splintering stone, the already battered angel statue snapped off its pedestal and tilted dangerously forward.

Nick realized it was falling straight toward where Carter was standing. With no time to shout out a

warning, he dove at his friend. In the same moment that he collided with Carter, shoving him out of the way, something heavy crashed down on Nick's back and slammed him into the ground. Lights flashed. He wasn't sure if they were from lightning or if they only existed in his head. Suddenly everything went black.

"Can you hear me?" Carter's voice pulled Nick from a woozy unconsciousness.

"Give him room," Angelo's voice said. "Don't crowd him."

Nick managed to lift one of his eyelids. "What happened?" he groaned. His voice sounded croaky and his whole body ached.

Carter's face appeared in front of Nick's open eye. "You saved my life, dude. And got kind of smushed."

Angelo shoved Carter out of the way and peered down at Nick. "How do you feel?"

Nick reached up to touch his face and pried open

his other eye. "Like Frankenstein used me for a trampoline. And I mean the monster, not the bully."

"Frankenstein was actually the name of the doctor who created the monster," Angelo said.

"Him, too." Nick licked his lips. His tongue felt like a block of hard, dry wood. Propping his hands on the ground, he pushed himself into a sitting position. Something creaked in his back and his right leg felt oddly twisted. Looking around, he saw the flat graveyard grass had been replaced by a gray, rocky landscape. "Where are we?"

Carter and Angelo turned and together stared into the distance—their faces more worried than Nick had ever seen them. Twisting his stiff neck, he saw what had drawn their attention. The dull gray land around them looked like something you'd see on the moon—flat expanses of rock and dirt without a single tree or bush to break things up. Two or three miles away though, the ground rose steeply to a towering stone bluff.

At the edge of the cliff, a black castle that looked straight out of an especially bad nightmare overlooked the valley floor. Windows flickered with red and orange light that made the castle appear to be on fire. Black spires stabbed the air like jagged blades.

Even from this distance, he could see stooped figures shambling down the winding road toward the castle gate.

"I guess those guys walking around aren't there to offer free video game tokens and beach towels," Nick said, trying to lighten the mood. Not even Carter laughed at his lame attempt at a joke.

"You think he knows we're here?" Carter asked.

Angelo rubbed a hand across his forehead. Despite the cold, damp air, he and Carter were both sweating. "If our entrance made half as much noise here as it did in the cemetery, I'm guessing he will soon enough. When we first arrived, I could swear some of those . . . *creatures* walking up and down the hill turned in our direction."

Overhead, the sky was a smudgy ash color that didn't look like either day or night. There was no sign of the sun anywhere and the air had a sort of musty smell—like a damp towel that had been shoved into a corner where it could never quite dry.

"I don't think we're on Earth," Nick said. It was a crazy thing to say. After all, where else could they be? And yet, both Angelo and Carter nodded, neither bothering to argue.

Grunting, Nick tried to push himself up. Carter and

Angelo had to grab his hands and pull. And even then, it took all of his strength to keep from falling down again. His spine felt like someone had pounded spikes through it, and when he tried taking a step, his hip made a weird *phit-t-t-t* sound.

"Dude," Carter said, "I didn't know zombies could—"

"It wasn't a fart," Nick said. "Something's messed up with my hip." He tried walking. Step. *Phit-t-t-t.* Step. *Phit-t-t-t.* Step. *Phit-t-t-t.* Step. *Phit-t-t-t.*

Carter put a hand over his mouth and snorted. Even when Nick glared at him, he couldn't stop giggling. "Sorry, it's just . . . it sounds like you've been eating beans for breakfast, lunch, and dinner. If we lit a match you could probably shoot all the way to the castle like a rocket."

"I told you, they aren't farts," Nick muttered. When he noticed that even Angelo was trying to hide a smile, he shook his head. "You two are totally warped."

Angelo and Carter burst into uncontrollable laughter. Soon even Nick found himself joining them. It was so wrong to be standing there with a broken body in an alien landscape, only a mile or two from likely death at the hands of a powerful zombie sorcerer, howling like an idiot. But somehow hearing himself and his friends laughing at it all made everything a little more bearable.

When the laughter had finally trickled away to a few stray snorts and an occasional hiccup, Carter wiped his eyes and said, "I seriously can't believe you saved my life, man."

Nick waved his hand. "You'd do the same thing for me. In fact, you did, coming here."

"So, what's the plan?"

Angelo pulled out his notes. "Grandma Elisheba said we take the amulet to the Zombie King. Once he gets it back, the curse will be removed from Nick."

"You really think it's going to be that simple?" Nick asked. "You think he'll just say 'Thanks for the amulet' and let us go home?"

Angelo chewed his thumbnail.

There were a lot of things that had been bothering Nick about this. "That old lady never told us why the Zombie King wants the amulet. She never told us what she was doing in Pleasant Hill when I saw her in Louisiana just the week before. You think it's a coincidence that she has a shop in the same town as us? And what's in it for her? She never asked for any kind of payment. Not even for the black salt."

"Those might have been good questions to bring up *before* we got sent to the Zombie King's castle," Carter said.

He was right. It was just that things had happened

so quickly. One minute they'd been performing a ceremony to take away his curse. The next minute he was a zombie for life. When the old woman had promised a way out, he hadn't been thinking clearly. Now it was too late.

The three boys stared silently at one another, all of their humor gone.

"You think you can make it that far?" Angelo asked, gazing up at the castle.

Nick put his hands on his friends' shoulders and began to walk. On his third step, something fell from a rip in his pants pocket and landed on the ground. It was his aunt's bottle. Angelo reached down to pick it up. Before he could, there was a cracking sound and the top of the bottle fell away.

"You broke it," Carter said.

Gray smoke hissed out of the tiny opening at the bottle's tip. It swirled uncertainly in the air for a moment before assuming a form Nick had seen only in pictures.

"Aunt Lenore?" he gasped.

"It's a ghost," Carter yelped.

Angelo held a finger to his lips. "I don't think it's a ghost. I think it's Lenore's spirit, her *gros-bon-ange*?"

Nick nodded silently.

The swirling gray figure looked around as if disoriented before focusing on Nick. "If my *pot tet* has opened, I must assume I am dead."

"Afraid so," Nick said.

Lenore's spirit turned to look at the castle in the distance. "We are in the realm of the Zombie King. How did this happen?"

Nick scratched at his sewn-on ear. "I found the amulet in your graveyard and kind of turned myself into a zombie."

Aunt Lenore gazed at him. "I always wanted to meet you. But I had hoped it would be under better circumstances." She looked at the cat and her lips pulled into a frown. "Isabelle, what have you and Elisheba been up to?"

Nick hadn't even realized Isabelle had come with them. *Great,* he thought, *my aunt's spirit is one of those old people that talks to cats.* He nearly fell over with shock when a girl's voice said, "What we needed to."

"Eep," Carter squeaked, jumping backward. "The cat talked."

Nick rubbed his hand across the top of his head. Things had been weird enough with zombies and skeletons, but this was just plain bizarre.

"You haven't introduced yourself, then?" Lenore

said, her mouth a dark hole in the shifting gray fog.

The cat twitched an ear in obvious irritation. "It didn't seem necessary."

"Okay, I'm freaking out here," Carter said, panting like a dog on a hot day. "Tell me that cat is not actually talking."

"No. I'm moving my mouth and you're imagining the rest." Isabelle glared at Carter with emotionless green eyes. "I'm warning you though, if you try to kick me or throw a single rock in my direction, I will scratch you so hard you'll think you got in a fight with a rosebush—and lost."

It was like one of those Disney movies where the animals talk and sing. Only Nick couldn't remember any of the animated creatures sounding quite this cranky. "Can someone tell me what's going on here?"

Aunt Lenore ran her fingers through her long gray hair. "The last thing I remember, Elisheba asked to meet me. We were drinking tea and I felt a sudden pain in my chest." She glared down at Isabelle. "She poisoned me, didn't she?"

The cat flicked her tail. "You didn't leave her much choice. You wouldn't give us the amulet and only another family member could open the vault."

Nick's mouth dropped open. "It wasn't the Zombie

King that needed me to go into the vault. It was the old woman." He'd been such an idiot.

"The witch," Carter growled. "If I could get my hands on that crazy old bat—"

"Careful what you say." Isabelle turned to look at the three boys. "That crazy old bat is my mother."

"Okay, now I'm seriously confused." Nick rubbed his aching leg. "Aunt Lenore is a spirit. You're a cat. Grandma Elisheba is a . . . well, I don't know exactly what she is. But I'm pretty sure she isn't a cat. How can she be your mother?"

Isabelle licked her front paw, smoothing a patch of ruffled fur into place. "That's a long story. We don't have time to tell it."

The smoke that was Aunt Lenore's spirit darkened. "We don't have time *not* to. You and your mother have put these boys in terrible danger. And I have some blame as well. The least we can do is to tell them what we've gotten them into." She looked at Nick's twisted leg. "Can you walk?"

"I think so," Nick said.

"Then we shall start toward the castle while I tell you what I can. The Zombie King is expecting us to bring him the amulet. It might be best to let him think that is your plan for as long as possible."

The imposing building gave Nick the shivers, but he followed his aunt, hoping she was right.

"Long before you were born," Lenore began, "a voodoo sorcerer arrived in the Louisiana bayou. He was always evil, but it wasn't until he came across an ancient amulet that he gained his true power."

Angelo, who had been writing furiously in his monster notebook, looked up. "The power to turn people into zombies?"

"That's right." Lenore nodded toward the horde of figures shuffling out of the castle gate in their direction. "The amulet gave the sorcerer the power to raise an army of the walking dead. And with each zombie he created, he became that much stronger, collecting their life essences in a green bottle, called an 'astral,' which he kept with him at all times."

Nick shivered at the thought. "How many?" he whispered.

"Hundreds," Lenore said sadly. "Maybe thousands."

Nick's mouth hung open. Carter stared. Even

Angelo stopped writing. *Thousands?* Thousands of people turned into zombies, their souls trapped forever?

"Didn't anyone try to stop him?" Carter asked.

Lenore waved a misty hand that drifted apart as it moved before drawing back together. "Many tried. Neighbors, other sorcerers, family members of those he had taken captive. Even the chief of police. But the bokor, who called himself the Zombie King, was mad with power. Anyone who opposed him was added to his army.

"Using his zombies as labor, he built himself a huge stone castle and plotted to take over the world. But he made one mistake. He allowed two seemingly innocent women to trick him into taking off his talisman. Without its protection, he was vulnerable. The life force in his astral was too strong for them to kill him. But they were able to trap him, his army, and his castle halfway between Earth and the underworld."

"Here?" Angelo whispered.

Isabelle and Lenore both nodded.

Nick stopped for a moment to catch his breath and rest his aching leg. "The two women, the ones who stopped the Zombie King. Was one of them you, Aunt Lenore? Were you a . . . voodoo queen?"

"I was," Lenore said. "But not in the way you think. The chief of police was my father. When he was captured by the Zombie King, I began to study everything I could find about dark magic. That's how I met Elisheba. I never intended to use it against anyone but the bokor, and I never did."

"Where do you come in?" Nick asked the cat.

Isabelle wound her tail about her legs. "I was only a girl at the time my mother and your aunt trapped the Zombie King. I followed them into the swamp that night to see what they were doing. I was too young to understand the danger. When I realized what they'd done, I was so excited I jumped out from my hiding place. Unfortunately, the Zombie King had one last trick before he was sent away. With the last of his power he turned me into a cat."

Nick rested his arm on Carter's shoulder to take away some of the pain in his hip. The zombies were so close now that he could make out their hungry eyes and slobbering faces. "Why a cat? Why didn't he change you into a zombie too?"

"He was too smart for that," Isabelle hissed. "If he'd changed me into a zombie, I would have been sucked down here with the rest of his army. Instead I was left to spend the rest of my life walking around on all fours,

lapping milk, and meowing. I was the perfect bargaining chip."

"We did everything we could to turn you back." Lenore's voice sounded like a breeze blowing through a swamp full of hanging tree moss.

"You didn't do enough." Isabelle's eyes flashed. "When my mother realized what the Zombie King had done to me, she wanted to give the amulet back right away. You wouldn't let her. You locked it in the crypt where no one but a blood relative could ever retrieve it."

"So you tricked me," Nick said to Isabelle. "You made me get turned into a zombie, so you and your mother could trade me to the Zombie King for your freedom."

"This is a really great story and all," Carter said, "but can you get us out of here before we end up being turned into zombie chow?" He pointed to the army of undead chomping their teeth hungrily.

Lenore's misty gray hair churned outward as she shook her head. "I am only a spirit. I have no power now."

Nick held out the broken bottle. "But Mazoo sent me your *pot tet*. He must have had a reason."

"The head jar was only intended as a way to keep my soul safe from the Zombie King. Mazoo should

have released it when I died. He must have thought you needed my counsel."

Angelo closed his notebook and glared at Isabelle. "How could you go along with something like that? How could you lead Nick into the cemetery, knowing what would happen there?"

The cat placed a paw over her eyes. "I was desperate. I knew if I didn't do it, I'd be stuck as a cat forever."

Nick's stomach burned. "That's no excuse. I'd do anything to get turned back from a zombie. But not if it meant someone else would be cursed."

Isabelle studied him. "No one made you go into the cemetery in Louisiana. You deliberately disobeyed your parents. And you actually *liked* being a zombie. I watched you use your powers to scare that boy in the woods."

Nick blinked. She was right. He *had* gone into the cemetery even though he knew it was wrong. He'd been thrilled to discover the amulet's power. If it hadn't been for his finger falling off, wouldn't he still be using it now? Scaring kids and pulling pranks? Maybe he *did* deserve whatever happened to him.

"Why did you do it?" Isabelle asked suddenly.

"What?" Nick had no idea what the cat was talking about.

"Why did you put yourself in harm's way when the statue was falling on Carter? Its weight could have destroyed you, zombie or not."

"I don't know," Nick said. It was true, he hadn't really thought about it. "I guess that's just what friends do. Look out for each other."

"Maybe it's time you thought about someone other than yourself for a change," Aunt Lenore told the cat. "It seems Mazoo was right. I am here to remind you that the selfishness of the Zombie King started all this in the first place. The only way to defeat him is by helping each other."

Isabelle twitched her whiskers and Nick could have sworn the cat smiled. A long, low note blasted through the air. The horde of shambling creatures was almost on top of them. They only had a minute or two at most to come up with a plan.

"What do we do?" Nick asked. "How do we get away?"

"You can't," Lenore said. "The only way to leave the Zombie King's realm is to destroy him. That would reverse all of his spells, including yours."

"How do you destroy a being so powerful?" Angelo asked.

Isabelle pawed at the ground as though thinking.

"There might be a way. Do you still have any of the black salt left?"

Angelo pulled the silk bag from his pocket and peered inside. "A little."

"What do we do, throw it on him?" Nick asked. That didn't sound too hard.

"No," Lenore said. "All that would do is make him angry. You've got to put it in his mouth. Black salt on his tongue will turn him to dust."

"That's just great!" Nick said. "How are we supposed to do that? Sprinkle it on a serving of scrambled brains?" It seemed hopeless. "Okay, give it to me," he said.

"No chance." Carter stepped forward and took the bag from Angelo. "You're a zombie too, in case you forgot. If it would turn him to dust, what do you think it would do to you? Besides, you're in no shape to do anything." Kneeling on the ground, he spit into the dust until it was wet enough to roll a small brown ball. He sprinkled the last of the black salt over the ball and kneaded it in.

"How are you going to get close enough to get that in his mouth?" Angelo asked, his eyebrows drawn low.

Carter shrugged. "I'm the smallest of us. No one ever suspects the little guy. But it wouldn't hurt if you could provide a distraction."

"What kind of distraction?" Angelo asked. Clearly things weren't going the way any of his books described.

"Think of something," Carter said. "Don't you always brag about how smart you are?"

The zombie army was so close now that Nick could smell their rotting bodies. "What's to keep the Zombie King from taking my amulet as soon as he sees me?"

"It doesn't work that way," Aunt Lenore said. "If he tries to take it from you or kill you, the amulet won't function for him. You have to give it to him. But don't do that. Once he has the amulet, he will never let you go and he will be free to turn the rest of the world into his own personal army of the undead."

Before Nick could ask any more questions, cold, bony hands closed around him, Angelo, and Carter.

Nick knew he stank. But compared to the stench of the army of shambling creatures herding him and his friends up the hill to the castle, he thought he smelled like roses.

"You guys ever heard of deodorant?" Carter asked the zombie closest to him. "Not just on your pits, either. If I were you, I think I'd buy about a dozen sticks and spread them all over my body."

The zombie turned a baleful silver eye on him, its other eye having disappeared at some point in the past. Nick was glad that at least that hadn't happened to him. He didn't think he could stand having Angelo sew his eyeball back in.

Angelo walked with his arms tucked close to his sides, his notebook clutched under one elbow. Nick didn't blame him. Being a zombie himself, he shouldn't have been as repulsed by the other undead as he was. But the thought of them touching him with their moldy bones and spongy flesh made him sick to his stomach.

Carter, on the other hand, appeared to be having a great time. "If any of you are thinking of eating my brain, don't bother," he called out. "I've been watching eight hours of TV every day since I was three. I'm sure I've rotted it completely away by now." Something fluttered out of his hand and fell to the ground. Before it disappeared under the feet of the zombie masses, Nick recognized it as a Snickers wrapper. Leave it to Carter to be eating at a time like this.

Nick noticed Aunt Lenore searching the faces of the undead army. Was she looking for her father?

"You think they remember what it was like to be human?" Nick asked.

"I doubt it," Angelo said. "I've been adding up the time in my head. If your great-aunt's father was trying to stop the Zombie King, I bet some of these guys have been zombies for almost fifty years."

Nick hadn't thought of that. Fifty years of being

under the control of a dark sorcerer—your mind and body weakening every day. "That thing Isabelle said," he told Angelo, "about us using the amulet to scare Frankenstein—I mean Cody. If I ever make it out of this alive, I'm going to tell him I'm sorry."

"You know he'll just beat you up," Angelo said.

"I know."

"I'll apologize with you," Carter said.

Nick looked over at him, wondering if he was joking. But he seemed sincere.

"Besides," Carter said, "after this, getting punched now and then doesn't seem that bad."

The rough dirt road they'd been following ended at the gate to the castle, and the zombies ahead of them moved aside. The boys stepped onto the gleaming black stone inside. Drafts of hot air blew across their faces, like the breath of a great black dragon.

"Use his ego against him if you can." Aunt Lenore's whispered voice was cold against Nick's ear. "He's not used to anyone opposing him."

The boys nodded. Nick hoped they'd get the chance. This close, the army of undead and the immense castle were more intimidating than he could have imagined. It was all he could do to keep putting one foot in front of the other.

The last of the zombies cleared a path in front of them and a set of long black steps appeared. At the top of the steps, a tall ebony throne glittered with dozens of precious gems. Seated in the throne was a man. His black cape and clothing blended into the throne so that his pale white face appeared to be floating in midair.

"Welcome to my humble home." The man's voice boomed and echoed. "How do you like it?"

Nick was too terrified to speak. But Carter called out, "Kind of got a thing for black going, huh? Have you ever considered purple or pink?" He pointed to the wall above the throne. "Maybe you could put a flat screen up there. Do they have zombie cable?"

The Zombie King seemed taken aback by Carter, but he quickly recovered. "You're a very funny little boy. I like you."

Carter held out his hands. "It's a talent. What can I say?"

Nick gaped at Carter. "What are you doing?" he whispered.

"I wonder if my pets will like you as much as I do?" The Zombie King snapped his fingers and a pair of huge black hounds raced from the sides of the hallway. Their skin hung from their ribs in flaps. Sharp white

teeth snapped and gnashed as the dogs charged toward Carter. All three boys tumbled backward and Isabelle's fur bristled in all directions.

At the last second, the zombie dogs skidded to a halt as though held on an invisible leash. But they continued to bark, their teeth flashing. Nick, Carter, and Angelo stood trembling as far away from the dogs as they could get without touching the zombies that had closed in behind them.

"That's more like it," the Zombie King said. "Children should learn to respect their elders, don't you think, my minions?"

A roar of "Yes, my King" filled the hall.

The Zombie King stood. His black cape flowed out behind him as he moved gracefully down the stairs. Unlike his army, his skin and hair appeared perfect and bone white. Nick wondered if it had something to do with the astral. His nose was thin and sharp, his cheeks like slabs of granite. His irises were so big they made his whole eyes look red.

He strode toward the boys, his hand gripping a scepter that burned with black flames, his head held high as though he really were a king. Nick could imagine people bowing before this man in terror. Several feet from the boys, he stopped and looked down at

Isabelle. “You have done well, my child.”

Isabelle pressed her small body against Nick’s ankles and gave a low hiss.

Ignoring her anger, the Zombie King turned to Nick and held out a palm as pale as his face. “I believe you have something for me.”

“You’ll never have it!” Aunt Lenore stepped out from behind the boys, her arms held wide. “Give up now and release these poor haunted souls.”

The Zombie King’s eyes went wide. With a snarl he swung his flaming scepter at Aunt Lenore. Scepter and hand went right through her, like a gust of wind splitting fog. For a moment he seemed shocked. Then he threw back his head and laughed, pointed teeth glittering. “I’d always hoped to kill you myself. But it seems someone has beaten me to it.”

“Well worth it to see that you are never returned to power,” Lenore said, and Nick felt his aunt’s courage seeping into him.

The zombies closed in behind Nick and his friends, forcing them forward. Their stench was overpowering. Stalling for time, Nick said, “How do I know you’ll change me back once I give you the amulet?”

The Zombie King lifted a single finger of his outstretched hand and bright green flame leaped from the

stone floor. "Step through this and you'll be good as new. Perhaps your friend should try it as well—it might cure his obnoxious mouth."

Carter snickered. "Nice one. You should have your own TV show."

The Zombie King glared at him.

Nick looked at the flames. The Zombie King couldn't kill him before he got the amulet back. What did he have to lose? He took a step forward, but the Zombie King lowered his finger and the flames disappeared. "*After* you give me the amulet," the bokor said.

Nick's fingers tightened around the amulet. He hoped Angelo and Carter came up with something soon.

"Don't do it!" Carter yelled. The Zombie King snarled at him. Carter gulped but kept talking. "You're totally not a jewelry guy. It doesn't work for you. Maybe a tattoo or something. You know, a—"

In an instant the Zombie King reached out and grabbed Carter by the throat. Lifting him so that the tips of his shoes barely touched the ground, he held him dangling. "I've had enough of your insolence." He turned to glare at Nick. "Give me the amulet now or your friend dies."

Nick started forward, but Angelo threw an arm out in front of him.

"Wait," Angelo said. "Don't hurt him and we'll give you the amulet."

The Zombie King released his grip enough so Carter could gasp for air.

"Here's the deal," Angelo said, his voice trembling. "Let me show you one thing first. Then the amulet is yours. Right, Nick?"

Nick nodded, wondering what Angelo was up to.

The Zombie King grimaced, his lips pressed tightly together. How were they ever going to get him to open his mouth enough to get the ball of black salt inside? "I'm losing my patience."

"It will only take a minute," Angelo said. "You've been waiting all these years. You can wait one more minute, can't you?"

"Very well," the bokor said. "What is it?"

"This is going to be great. You'll love this." Angelo patted his pockets as if looking for something. "Okay, I just need a worm and a glass of chocolate milk."

"What!" the Zombie King burst out.

"Chocolate milk," Angelo said. "I need a glass of chocolate milk and a worm to show you this."

"I'm not playing any more games," the Zombie King

said. "Give me the amulet now."

"His ego," Aunt Lenore whispered.

Nick took the amulet from his pocket. At the sight of it, the zombies moaned, pushing toward its red gem. The Zombie King reached out, his eyes glowing. But Nick held it over his own head like he was going to put it on himself. He had no clue what Angelo was up to, but if it required a worm and chocolate milk, then he would get it. "You promised. Give him what he needs or I swear you will never touch this. Unless you *can't* do it."

"I can do *anything*!" the Zombie King growled. He snapped his fingers. "Bring me a worm and . . . a . . . a glass of *chocolate milk*."

Nick had no idea where they got them, but a moment later two zombies limped forward. One held a slightly smeared glass of what looked like the most disgusting chocolate milk ever. The second held a worm coated with something slimy and green.

Angelo took the glass with a weak grin. He wiped the worm on his shirt, trying to remove the green stuff. If this was his distraction, it was working, Nick thought. It was definitely distracting him.

"Watch closely," Angelo said, his face nearly as pale as the Zombie King's. "You've never seen anything like this before."

Holding the wriggling worm in one hand, he took a big gulp of the chocolate milk. A second later he did something Nick would never have imagined from him. He popped the worm into his mouth.

"That's it?" The Zombie King chuckled. "You wanted me to see you eat a *worm*? I've seen men eat their own hearts. I've seen men devour—"

Angelo held up one finger, cutting the Zombie King off in mid-sentence. He put both hands over his ears, puffed out his cheeks, and . . . exploded.

At least that's what it sounded like. Chocolate milk spewed out of his nose in two brown streams. It was truly incredible. But that wasn't all. A second later, he reached into his right nostril with his thumb and forefinger and pulled out the worm—still wriggling.

Nick's mouth dropped open in surprise. So did the Zombie King's.

At that moment, Carter's hand shot forward. It was perfect. Angelo's distraction had done exactly what it needed to. The Zombie King's mouth hung wide-open. Carter's fingers uncurled to reveal the brown ball. He shoved it toward the Zombie King's lips.

Like a striking snake, the bokor reached out and

caught Carter's wrist. He squeezed until the ball dropped from Carter's fingers to the floor. Carter cried out in pain.

"Very amusing," the Zombie King said. "Now you will give me the amulet or I will tear your friend apart piece by piece."

The Zombie King twisted Carter's right arm until he screamed.

"Okay!" Nick held out the amulet. "Stop hurting him."

Easing back on Carter's arm ever so slightly, the bokor released his scepter. It floated in the air, black flames dancing. He held out his hand to Nick. "Give it to me."

"I don't care what you do with me," Nick said, his eyes blurring with tears. "But promise you'll let my friends go and turn Isabelle back into a girl."

"The time for promises has passed. Give me the amulet or watch your friends die agonizing deaths." He pointed a finger at his floating scepter and the flames drew out like sizzling black hands, reaching toward Carter's eyes.

"Stop!" Nick threw him the amulet. "Here. Take it." Despite everything he'd tried, he'd failed. And now because of him, his friends were going to be zombies forever.

The Zombie King caught the amulet. His mouth drew back in a greedy smile. "At last." He looped the chain around his neck and the gem at the center of the amulet flared bright red. The zombies surged toward the amulet's light.

Nick looked down at his body, waiting to become human again.

"It takes a few hours to change back," the Zombie King said. "Unfortunately, you don't have that much time."

Hands closed around Nick's arms and legs. At the same time, zombies grabbed Angelo and Isabelle. Nick struggled, but the undead hands held him tightly. "What are you doing?" he screamed, trying to pull away from the scabby hands that clutched at his body.

"I will turn your friends into my mindless servants," the Zombie King said with a wicked sneer. "I'm sure it will amuse Elisheba to see her daughter returned to her—as a drooling zombie. Perhaps I'll even let her become one herself. But not you. As Lenore is no longer alive, I'm afraid I will have to take out the revenge meant for her on you."

"Please," Lenore begged. "You have what you want. Let him go."

"What I want is to see him suffer the way I've longed to make you suffer." The bokor motioned to the brown ball lying on the floor. A zombie reached down and picked it up. Another pair of zombies grabbed Nick's jaws. Bony fingers with slivers of stinking flesh forced his mouth open. "No!" he screamed when he realized what they were going to do.

"Allow him to experience the fate he had in store for me," the Zombie King said.

Nick twisted left and right trying to get free.

"Let him go!" Angelo shouted. Isabelle scratched and clawed, hissing and growling, but couldn't escape. Aunt Lenore swung her insubstantial limbs. Only Carter—perhaps in shock—remained silent.

The zombie holding the brown ball stopped in front of Nick. The Zombie King watched intently, his eyes glittering with pleasure.

Slowly, the undead creature forced the ball between Nick's lips. Nick tried to clench his teeth—to force the

ball away with his tongue—but the zombies were too strong. As soon as the clay was completely inside his mouth, the undead holding his jaws forced them shut.

Nick closed his eyes, waiting for his body to disintegrate into a million particles of dust. When nothing happened, he opened his eyes. He looked at Angelo, who shook his head, then at Carter. Amazingly, his friend grinned and winked.

The Zombie King opened his mouth in amazement. In that second, Carter brought up his left hand. Somehow it also held a brown ball. Before the Zombie King could react, Carter jammed it between the bokor's lips and shouted, "The Three Monsterteers!"

The Zombie King had one startled moment of surprise before his body exploded into a whirling cloud of sand. At the same moment, the amulet burst into millions of tiny red rays of light. The sand swirled in the air for a moment before settling on the ground in a small white mound.

"I told him he would have been better off with a tattoo," Carter said.

Without the leader to guide them, the zombies released their hold on Nick and he dropped to the ground. Nick spit the ball into his hand. "What . . . ?" he started to ask before seeing what was in his palm. Now

that he was no longer terrified, he could taste it as well.

"I don't understand," Angelo said, looking from the ball in Nick's hand to the pile of white dust that had been the zombie king. "If you had the black salt ball in your left hand all along, what did they put in Nick's mouth?"

Carter laughed. "I call it the Snickers bar offensive."

Angelo smiled widely. "You rolled up the candy bar."

"You did it!" a voice squealed.

The three boys turned to see a girl about their age. She was wearing a plain white dress. Curly hair the exact color of the cat's fur flowed across her shoulders.

"Isabelle?" Nick asked.

She nodded excitedly. "I thought I'd be older now. But I guess the curse didn't work that way. Look at me," she said waving her arms. "I'm human."

Carter, Angelo, and Nick, who weren't particularly experienced talking to pretty girls, nodded awkwardly.

Isabelle dropped to her knees and sifted through the pile of white sand. After a few seconds of digging, she pulled out a green bottle. "Do you mind?" she asked Nick.

"Not at all."

Isabelle lifted the green astral above her head. Something inside glimmered for a moment as though

sensing its impending freedom. Then she brought it down and smashed the bottle on the stone floor of the castle. A thousand moans of relief sounded at the same time. The zombies' dull, witless faces lit up.

One of them looked a little like Nick's father. Aunt Lenore flew toward the zombie, crying, "Father!" She threw her arms around the man's neck just as the entire undead army disappeared with a whoosh—freed at last to fulfill their own destinies.

A second later, Lenore disappeared too. As she did, Nick could have sworn he heard a soft *"Thank you."*

Isabelle turned to Carter. "That was brilliant. I had no idea you were capable of something like that."

Carter blushed. "It was just, you know, I, well, um . . ."

Isabelle stepped toward him. "You were wonderful!"

Carter backed away. His face, which had already been pink before, now flushed a red nearly as brilliant as the Zombie King's amulet. The world around them swirled, like paint going down a drain. Isabelle reached toward Carter, but before her fingers could touch him, they all disappeared.

• • •

Nick blinked. They were in the cemetery again, near the broken angel statue. In the east, the sky was beginning to turn from black to purple. "We're home," he said with a sigh.

Carter reached down to touch the grass as if making sure it was real. "That was the most scared I've ever been in my life."

"It was definitely a close call," Angelo agreed. He looked down at his monster notebook, and Nick could see his friend mentally cataloging all the new information he'd need to add to it.

"I seriously thought life as we knew it was over," Nick said.

"No kidding." Carter touched his cheek. "I think she was going to hug me." The thought of being hugged by a girl other than possibly their moms was too weird for any of them to imagine.

Nick took a deep breath. His heart was still pounding from— *Wait!* His heart was *pounding.* His lungs were inhaling and exhaling. "Look," he said, holding out his hand. The stitches where his finger had been sewn on were gone. "I'm human again." He walked in a circle. His leg and back felt fine and there was no farting sound anymore.

"I wonder if Isabelle's back with her mom?" Carter

asked. "Not that I care or anything. Just curious."

Nick laughed and clapped him on the back. "You are such a lady's man. I think you *wanted* her to hug you."

Carter balled up his fists. "Take that back or I swear . . ."

Angelo stepped between them, putting a hand on each of his friends' shoulders. "I think we've had enough fighting for one day. We need to get home before our parents realize we've been out all night. Besides, don't forget, we were going to apologize to Cody today."

"About that," Carter said. "I'm thinking maybe I'll let the two of you handle talking to Frankenstein by yourselves."

"There you are," a girl's voice called.

Nick turned, expecting to see Isabelle. Instead he saw Angie, Dana, and Tiffany pushing their way through a thick stand of bushes. The three girls were wet and covered with grass and mud stains from head to foot.

"Now we've got you," Dana said.

"And we know what you are." Tiffany pushed a strand of hair out of her face. Nick had never seen her look so messy.

Carter crinkled his nose. "What happened to you three?"

"What *happened*?" Dana shouted. "What happened is that we've been following you all night. We saw you enter that voodoo shop. We saw you go into the cemetery. And just as we were about to catch up with you it was like the entire graveyard exploded!"

Angelo looked around. "It seems pretty quiet now."

"Stop pretending." Angie stomped up to Nick. "It took me a while to put it all together. But we've figured it out. Not breathing. Cold and clammy. Cuts not healing. That amulet you wore at the pool. And then I realized what must have happened at dinner. You are a *zombie*!"

"A what?!" Nick asked, as though that were the nuttiest thing he'd ever heard.

"An undead zombie. And I can prove it." Angie put a hand on his cheek. "See, your skin is . . . *warm*." She pulled her fingers away, looking at her palm as though she couldn't believe what she'd felt.

Nick grinned. "I think you three girls need to stop watching so many monster movies."

"Maybe you should cut back on Halloween candy, too." Carter chuckled. "In fact, maybe you shouldn't go out on Halloween at all."

Angie shook her head. "I was *sure*." She looked so disappointed, it was all Nick could do not to tell her the

truth, as she and her friends turned and started back toward the cemetery gates.

"Better not go to the football game next Friday night," Angelo called after them. "I hear the other team's players are *monsters*."

The three girls turned back and glared. "You think you got away with something, Braithwaite," Angie said, "but I'm watching you."

"Let's go." Nick laughed as he and his friends walked toward their bikes. It had been pretty cool being a zombie. Not as cool as a werewolf or a vampire, maybe. But still cool. He had to admit though, he was glad everything was back to normal.

"Pardon me," a voice called.

Nick turned to see Alabaster, the fat ghost with the hat, hurrying to catch up with him. Carter and Angelo kept walking as though neither of them had heard or seen anything.

"About that pastrami sandwich," the ghost said, licking his thick, transparent lips.

Okay, so maybe not *completely* normal.

A Final Warning

I see you survived, as did Nick and his friends. And yet I have a feeling their case is not even nearly closed. Things are changing in Pleasant Hill, returning to their older—less *pleasant*—ways. Why, just the other day, I noticed a man digging in the cemetery late at night. I wonder what he could have been looking for?

But that's a story for another day.

Be careful. Until then, if you notice odd howls coming from the woods nearby, eyes peering from the dark, or strange symbols scrawled on the sidewalk in what you hope is only red paint, it might be best to ignore them. Or my next case file could be about you.

Sincerely,

B. B.

ACKNOWLEDGMENTS

Most people think those of us who dabble in the world of the undead, newly dead, or never lived spend all of our time in creepy, spider-infested cellars, poring over ancient tomes and dissecting bodies. Well, that is perfectly true. However, on the rare occasions when we seek to share our stories with the rest of the world, we must play nicely with others. With that in mind, there are a few . . . um, *creatures,* I must thank for the amazing things they did to put this novel in your hands.

First, I must recognize the talent, brilliance, and insight of the Literary Lord of the Night, Michael Bourret. If it wasn't for his insight and encouragement, this story would still be moldering on my shelves with classics like *Bones—They're Not Just for Breakfast Anymore* and *Ten Things to Do with Grave Moss.* The undead world kneels at your spiked boots, Michael, and I say this not only because I want you to keep sending me gruel.

Those who bring the undead to life often tend to remain in the shadows. However, even bokors need

to step out from their vaults at times. His Darkness Andrew Harwell took my scrabbled scribbles and turned them into something I am proud to see the light of day. You are absolutely amazing, and I thank you from the bottom of my nonbeating heart for your vision, imagination, and hard work. An undead could not be luckier than to have you pulling their strings.

In a row of cages beneath my operating table, I keep creatures so foul, smelly, and vile that they are the only things I can entrust to slobber over my words and tell me if they work or not. To these rapaciously reading wretches I give my sincere thanks—and an extra slug at mealtime: Jonathan and Katherine Eden; Zach Staheli; Megan Lyon; Dana Moore; Calvin Condie; Robin, David, Connor, and Brennen Weeks; the Clement family; the Blackhurst family; Mark and Maria Savage; and Dick and Vicki Savage.

Far away from here is a dark and forbidding swamp known as Harpervania, where creatures of the night shamble to and fro at a surprisingly fast pace, completing tasks so vile, so heinous, I barely dare utter their names, lest I find them slavering over my rotting corpse one night. But speak of them I must, for their acts made this book all it could be and more: Sarah Kaufman,

whose wicked designs amaze even me, Doug Holgate, whose brilliantly evil drawings bring my words to life; and Barbara Lalicki, who can change the world (for the better) with a wave of her gris-gris pen. To them and all the other dwellers of Harpervania, thank you. I am unworthy of your dark talents.

I truly question whether I should mention this denizen of the darkest portals. Few demons are as dangerous (or rank-smelling). And yet, despite his foul visage and less than optimal hygiene, he has become a great friend and mentor over the years. So thanks, James Dashner.

No true worker of wickedness would be complete without a coven of fellow scribblers. With a word of apology to all the other covens out there, mine is the best. Their writings and works have sustained me for more than a decade, and I would be lost in the Dungeons of Despair without their encouragement and friendship. Give it up for Sarah Eden, Michele Holmes, Annette Lyon, Heather Moore, Lu Ann Staheli, and Robison Wells.

I saved the most important for last. Surely no worker of the evil arts, delving where living beings dare not go, could ever hope to have a family. And yet,

somehow, crawling through graveyards, recording the screeches of the terrifying, and notating the life cycle of the unbelievable, I have four minions and a bride of darkness always at my side. Thanks and (un)dying gratitude to Nightshade Nicholas, Jacobas Giganticus, Scott the Devourer, Erica the Evil, and she who commands all, Jennifer the Magnificent. You guys are my life, such as it is.